CONTENTS

Acknowledgments

Dedication

ONE   2

TWO   25

THREE   45

FOUR   66

FIVE   89

SIX   113

SEVEN   134

EIGHT   159

NINE   180

TEN   204

ELEVEN   228

EPILOGUE   260

Author's Note   268

The Corgi Case Files Series   270

CORGI CASE FILES

Case of the
Chatty Roadrunner

Corgi Case Files, Book 6

J.M. Poole
www.AuthorJMPoole.com

Sign up for Jeffrey's newsletter on his website
to get all the latest corgi news

True happiness is being owned by a corgi!

Case of the Chatty Roadrunner
Published by Secret Staircase Books, an imprint of
Columbine Publishing Group, LLC
PO Box 416, Angel Fire, NM 87710

Book layout and design by Secret Staircase Books
Cover images by Yevgen Kachurin, Irisangel, Felipe de Barros

First Secret Staircase paperback edition: January 2021
First Secret Staircase e-book edition: January 2021

* * *

Publisher's Cataloging-in-Publication Data

Poole, J.M.
Case of the Chatty Roadrunner / by J.M. Poole.
p. cm.
ISBN 978-1649140296 (paperback)
ISBN 978-1649140302 (e-book)

1. Zachary Anderson (Fictitious character)--Fiction. 2. Pomme Valley,
Oregon (fictitious location)—Fiction. 3. Phoenix, Arizona—Fiction.
4. Amateur sleuth—Fiction. 5. Pet detectives—Fiction. I. Title

Corgi Case Files Mystery Series : Book 6.
Poole, J.M., Corgi Case Files mysteries.

BISAC : FICTION / Mystery & Detective.
813/.54

ACKNOWLEDGMENTS

The long-awaited resolution to the death of Zachary's wife is finally here! At long last, we finally learn just what did happen to Zachary's late wife, Samantha. Was it merely an accident, as everyone had originally thought, or was foul play involved?

This story is the result of the overwhelming support of the fans and their desire to see further adventures of Zack and the dogs. This marks the 6th story in the series, and you'll be pleased to know, there are more on the way. So, without further ado, I'd like to thank some people for their help in creating this book.

The cover was again illustrated by a talented artist from Brazil by the name of Felipe de Barros. He's done 5 of the 6 titles thus far, and I hope to use him for all future volumes in the Corgi Case Files series.

I'd like to thank the members of my Posse for helping polish up the book. You know who you guys are, but most specifically, Jason, Carol, Elizabeth, and Diane. You guys and gals do an admirable job in preventing me from looking like a horse's ass. :)

As always, I am forever grateful to my loving

wife, Giliane, who continues to prove to me that she's the hardest worker I have ever known. And for my little Keeley... I'll never forget you, pup. Until we meet again.

J.

For Keeley —

If not for you, pup, this series would never have started. You left us much too soon and left me with a sizeable hole in my heart. Be at peace, sweet girl. Run free until we meet again!

ONE

T his has got to be the most messed up, idiotic, poorly planned airport I have ever had the misfortune of seeing in my entire life. I mean, how the hell do we get out of here? Did you see any signs that said 'exit'? I didn't. There's a sign that says 44th St. There's one that says Buckeye. What the hell is a buckeye, anyway? I'm telling you, man, it's enough to drive anyone insane."

"Well, you just passed an exit, pal. And ... there goes another one. Tell me again why you didn't want me to drive?"

"Everyone knows you have a lousy sense of direction, Zack. There's no way I'm letting you behind the wheel."

"Even though this is my hometown? Seriously?"

"Vance?" a female voice hesitantly asked. "Are you sure you wouldn't like Zachary to drive?"

"I'm a police officer," Vance crossly reminded us. "It's impossible for me to get lost."

"Tell that to the corn maze from last year," I

reminded my friend. "You were just as lost then as you are now."

"Am not."

"Stay in the far left lane," I instructed. We had just passed Terminal 3, after looping around for the third time, and were approaching another exit. "The next time you see a sign for 44th Street, take it. We can take that all the way up to Camel-back."

All right. Let's catch you up. Vance, Jillian, and I, along with Sherlock and Watson, had just arrived in Arizona, with the intent to look into my late wife's death. Now, as a former resident of Phoenix, I'll admit the act of leaving the Phoenix International Airport with your sanity intact can be tricky for those not familiar with its layout. I had no idea my friend Vance, police detective extraordinaire, would get so turned around that we'd end up circling the airport like vultures over road kill. I glanced back at the dogs. Neither were willing to look at me. Hell, I couldn't blame them.

Let me explain.

After the flight had landed, while Vance arranged ground transportation, I had moseyed over to the Customer Service desk to pick up the dogs, who unfortunately, had to ride in the cargo hold. I knew both wanted out of the crate, but I wasn't about to let them out in the airport, so they were going to have to suffer in silence for a bit longer. Since both were in the same large crate, gazing at me with what had to be the worst case of corgi stink eye I had ever seen, I had to either carry the crate or come up with another option. Thankfully, it presented itself in the form of those rentable airport trolleys. The dogs were still angry with me, but now that they could see us, both appeared to be settling down.

I really couldn't blame them. I had tried everything I could think of, short of bribery, to get the airline to allow the dogs in the cabin with me. Apparently, their rule was if the dog and the crate could both fit under the seat in front of you, then they'd allow it. For an additional fee, of course. Plus, they'd only allow a certain number of dogs in the main cabin, so you had to hope they'd have an opening or two.

Well, in this case, the corgis were just too big. So, after both airline employees assured me that the cargo cabin was temperature controlled, and quite safe, and even produced pictures to back up their claims, I relented and agreed to put the dogs in the cargo hold. It was either that or else we were going to have to drive, and take it from someone who has made that particular drive before, I wasn't looking for a repeat performance.

Once we were in Vance's rental car, which turned out to be a mini-van, much to my amusement, we were off. Only, we didn't make it far. Navigating your way through unfamiliar territory can be frustrating, I'll admit, and the Phoenix International Airport could hopelessly confuse even the most directionally-inclined locals. Out-of-towners didn't have a chance.

Finally, with my help, we were putting some distance between us and the airport. We were heading north now, on 44th Street, when Jillian pulled out the brochure she had printed online about the hotel we booked. It was a place called The Phoenician. Even though I used to live in the city, and I had heard of the hotel before, I had never once stayed there. Why? 'Cause the sucker was a luxury resort and the price tag had been way too high for my liking. However, either I had to pony up the money for my share or else Jillian told me she'd just take care of the bill herself. Well, as you can imagine, no, that wasn't gonna happen.

Darn it.

Anyway, the reason we're here is that two months ago, I received a phone call from a woman I didn't know, who claimed my late wife, Samantha, hadn't died in an accident as I had originally thought. Instead, this mystery lady claimed it was premeditated and had been trying to get a message to me for some time about it.

For those of you who may not be familiar with my late night phone calls, let me explain. Practically every night, at 3:30 in the friggin' morning, my phone would ring. There was never any caller ID, nor was there anyone on the line. However, that came to a screeching halt after I was told Samantha's death wasn't an accident.

Since my late night phone calls had come to an abrupt stop, I knew I had to look into the matter. Therefore, I hired a local private investigator in Phoenix, one by the name of Alex Stokes, to do some digging. Well, he apparently had found something that corroborated my mystery woman's claims, because he requested I return to Phoenix and go over whatever he had found.

My new girlfriend, Jillian Cooper, also from Pomme Valley and owner of Cookbook Nook, as well as our good friend Vance Samuelson, Pomme Valley's finest police detective, and my two dogs, Sherlock and Watson, all came with me to Arizona to sort this mess out. I didn't know what we were going to find, but let me tell you, I was so glad I had their support. You see, I wasn't too sure how I was going to handle this. Why? For the simple reason I hadn't stepped foot back in Arizona since I had moved away, which was almost immediately after Samantha's death.

So, with my friends and my dogs in tow, I was back in my old hometown to discover, once and for all, what had happened to my beloved Samantha. If she really was murdered, then you had better believe I wanted to see whoever was responsible behind bars. For life.

"This place looks really nice!" Jillian observed, as we pulled into the resort's main drive.

"I'll say," as I gazed admiringly at the freshly cut lawn and the meticulously landscaped grounds. "At least the dogs aren't barking. I don't know what was bugging them earlier, but Sherlock just wouldn't stop woofing. What was it, every ten minutes or so? Anyway, just look at this place. I've always wanted to stay here, but I never got around to it. Something about trying to justify forking over that much money when I lived less than thirty minutes away. Anyway, I don't know about this. Are you sure they take pets? I don't ever remember the Phoenician stating they allowed dogs before."

"Well, they do," Jillian confirmed. "Their website clearly states that there are a limited number of pet friendly rooms, and they'll accommodate up to two dogs at no more than 40lbs each."

I turned in my seat to regard Sherlock and Watson, who were resting on the floor of the van. Sherlock looked up at me just as I spun in my seat. Thankfully, neither corgi was overweight, which was a common problem for the smallest member of the herding group. Corgis always acted like they were starving, so overfeeding happened a lot. Not to my dogs, though. My two corgis were sleek, energetic, and fit as a fiddle. They were both intelligent, inquisitive, and sharp as tacks. Anyone familiar with my dogs know full well they are more than likely smarter than I am. Sherlock, for example, has solved more homicide cases than most of the detectives on the Pomme Valley police force. Sadly, that included Vance, but that's a sore subject and one I don't typically bring up.

As we pulled into the front entrance, a uniformed member of the hotel staff, complete with white gloves, opened the door for us. As we unloaded our stuff, I couldn't help but notice both dogs had zeroed in on the staff member and were watching the young man like a hawk. Was there a reason?

The uniformed employee finally caught sight of the dogs, smiled broadly, and squatted. He reached behind his back and, when he was sure both dogs were watching, produced two doggie biscuits. Both corgis sat, on cue.

"Aren't you two some of the cutest dogs I have ever seen?" the teenager gushed. "Here you go."

"You just made two friends for life," I observed, with a chuckle.

"What are their names?" the employee asked.

I pointed to the dog closest to him, "That one is Sherlock, with the red, white, and black on him. On your left is Watson."

"Sherlock and Watson? That's clever!"

We were led into the resort's posh lobby, where polished marble gleamed in all four corners of the room. I saw statues reclining in various poses scattered around the room. Colorful paintings depicting various countrysides, resplendent in their golden frames, were on every wall. Every wall that didn't have a window, that is, because directly behind the check-in counter was a wall of nothing but windows overlooking the Salt River Valley.

And the view! Wow! I've lived in Arizona for many years, but I have never tired of seeing the beauty of the desert. Yeah, I know that sounds weird, but until you've visited the desert and are able to see for yourself what I'm talking about, then you shouldn't brand me crazy. Well, not yet, anyway.

There's something about being able to look out at the rugged beauty, with no signs of civilization anywhere, in conditions that should make quality of life an absolute nightmare. However, I don't think I've ever seen more wildlife than I have in Arizona. Rabbits, quail, coyotes, lizards, and even lynx are some of the critters you may encounter. But, for every silver lining, you'll always find a dark side, and Arizona has some of the nastiest critters too. Rattlesnakes, scorpions, tarantulas, and sun spiders, to name a few.

Eww. Sun spiders. Don't get me started on those mean, aggressive little SOBs. Imagine a tailless scorpion with an attitude. They loved getting out of the sun, and once they set their sights on getting into your house, you had better be prepared with a can of Raid. And a lighter.

Anyway, once I realized I was bringing the dogs with me to Arizona, I vowed never to let them out of my sight. It just wasn't worth the risk. So, either they stay in the room, or in this case, casita, or they accompany me, and since I was trying to solve a mystery, you'd better believe I planned on having them by my side at all times.

Once we were checked into our casitas, and Jillian had persuaded me to unpack my luggage into the available dressers, we were ready to meet my private investigator.

Alex Stokes was a life-long resident of the Grand Canyon State. He claimed that he has solved hundreds of cases, ranging from traffic infractions, to settling domestic disputes, to even locating missing family members, whether they wanted to be found or not. His website stipulated that if he couldn't produce desired results, then his fee would drop to a paltry 10% of the final bill. In my mind's eye, that was definitely worth a shot.

While Jillian and I were chatting about Lentari Cellars, and the latest award Caden had managed to win on my behalf, there was a knock on the door. I opened it and ushered in a man in his early thirties. He had brown hair, was about six inches shorter than I was, and seemed to be in reasonable shape. He wore nondescript clothing, which consisted of a simple gray polo and a pair of blue jeans. He carried a worn leather briefcase, which had several scratches and scuff marks on it, suggesting he might have used it to clock someone over the head a few times.

As I studied the P.I., it dawned on me how perfect Alex Stokes looked. By that, I mean, here was someone who could easily blend in without being noticed. There was nothing remarkable in his appearance which would stand out; therefore, he was perfect for this type of work.

"Mr. Anderson," Alex said, by way of greeting. He shook my hand.

"This is my girlfriend, Jillian Cooper," I said, giving Jillian's hand a light squeeze, "and over there is Vance Samuelson. He's my detective friend I told you about."

Alex nodded appreciatively. "I'm glad you're here, Mr. Anderson."

"Please," I scoffed. "Call me Zack."

"Very well, Zack. As you know, I have uncovered some developments that I thought you should know about."

"What kind of developments?" Vance asked, as he reached for his notebook.

"How much do you know?" Alex asked, as he turned to face Vance. "Has Mr. Anderson, er, Zack, told you the circumstances of his wife's death?"

Vance nodded. "Yes. I know she was in her vehicle, and for some reason, it veered into oncoming traffic, where it struck a semi-truck head on. Death was instantaneous."

"What have you discovered?" I asked.

Jillian took my hand in hers, patted it a few times, and then looked over at Vance.

"What do you say we have lunch first?" she suggested. "I know Zachary hasn't eaten anything since first thing this morning. I think it would be better."

Vance laid a friendly hand on my shoulder and then looked at the P.I. for confirmation. When Alex indicated he didn't have any problem with going to lunch first, we all headed for the door. However, we were brought up short when two corgis materialized out of nowhere and blocked access to the casita's front door.

"Awwooooo!" Sherlock howled. Then the corgi looked pointedly at Alex. I couldn't help but grin.

"Sorry, Alex. This is Sherlock and Watson, both of whom do not like to be left out of the introductions. Sherlock? Watson? This is Alex Stokes. He's the investigator looking into Samantha's death."

Since neither dog had on a leash, both corgis were able to approach the P.I., where they sat at his feet and looked up at him. Alex saw that he was being watched, smiled warmly at the dogs, and held out a hand. Sherlock didn't waste any time giving the hand a lick. Neither did Watson, for that matter.

"Welcome to the pack," I announced.

"Cute dogs," Alex decided. "How long have you had them?"

"Since I moved to Oregon," I answered. "I never planned on getting a dog, but these two were practically dropped in my lap, and do you know what? I couldn't be happier."

Once we were seated at one of the resort's eight restaurants, namely J&G Steakhouse, Alex opened his briefcase and started rifling through it. Then he pulled out a notebook and began to read.

"Samantha Masters Anderson, pharmaceutical sales rep for Semzar Pharmaceuticals. Of all the hundred or so sales reps the company employed, she was in the top five percent for the last three years. Whether or not that earned her any enemies remains to be seen."

I nodded. "She was good at her job, no doubt

about it. She could sell ice to an Eskimo. I will admit I didn't know she was one of the top per-formers. I wonder how many people they have working there. Maybe someone thought she was stepping on some toes?"

"Did you have any idea what your wife was selling?" Alex asked, as he started taking his own notes.

I shrugged. "I would imagine whatever drugs Semzar was currently manufacturing. She never really told me, since Sam knew I wasn't interested in all those new-fangled drugs."

"And all their side effects," Jillian added.

Vance nodded. "That's true. Just about all the ads nowadays spend more time talking about what *could* happen instead of what *will* happen."

Alex made a few more notes.

"Is that relevant?" I asked, confused.

Alex nodded. "It is, yes."

"How?" Vance wanted to know.

Alex reached into his briefcase and pulled out a glossy brochure. Clearly visible along the top of the brochure were the words Semzar Pharmaceut-icals. He handed me the brochure and tapped the topic sentence:

REVOLUTIONARY DIABETES DRUG ON THE CUSP OF APPROVAL FROM THE FDA!

"Glucosoquin is rapidly becoming the flagship drug of choice that every sales rep wishes they were selling," the P.I. told me. "According to this, glucosoquin has been proven to prevent diabetes."

Jillian nodded appreciatively. "That's wonderful news! I know several people who will be happy to hear that."

"It gets better," Alex informed us. "Glucosoquin doesn't require any change in diet, nor does it require any amount of exercising to work. All you have to do is take one pill every single day."

Vance's mouth dropped open. "You're kidding! Holy cow. Those guys are going to make a fortune! Do you know how many people are going to want to get their hands on that medicine?"

I tapped the brochure. "Wait, are you telling me this is what Samantha was selling?"

Alex nodded. "Yes. She was one of three representatives that were pre-selling the drug to hospitals, clinics, and private practices for trial runs."

I leaned back in my chair and contemplated what I had just heard. Had Samantha told me anything about this new drug? Sadly, if she had, then it had been long forgotten. I, unfortunately, had a habit of tuning out bits of information I didn't understand. And, as luck would have it, that included Samantha's work. Now, before you start thinking I'm the most insensitive husband on the face of the planet, I should inform you that Sam knew all about my propensity for ignoring her. True, she didn't care for it, but then again, she really didn't press the issue. She knew being a pharmaceutical sales rep wasn't always the most fascinating of jobs, but hey, it helped pay the bills. Come to think of it, there were quite a few times when her share of the income easily outweighed my own. Those huge corporations gave out bonuses on a regular basis, so who was I to argue?

I was starting to feel sick to my stomach. Had there been some type of problem at Sam's work, and I hadn't paid enough attention to discover it? Clearly, Sam had ruffled a few feathers by being able to sell this new, popular pharmaceutical. Well, if this was the case, it should be easy enough to prove. With Sam out of the picture, we just had to find out who had replaced her. Who had Semzar Pharmaceuticals allowed to take Samantha's place?

"What are you thinking?" Jillian asked.

"I was thinking that we ought to go talk to Semzar. If only a few people were allowed to sell this super-popular drug, then I can only assume the wait-list, so to speak, must have been long. Who took her place on that list? That's what I want to know."

"If the FDA hadn't approved the drug yet," Vance said, as he scribbled notes, "then how would they be able to sell the drug? It's not like they'd be allowed to use it, right?"

Alex shrugged. "They could if they were in another country. As you know, Mexico is only a few hours away. People have also gone to Canada to get procedures done that aren't allowed here in the US yet."

"Would the patient then have to return to the country of administration should they need a follow-up?"

Alex shook his head. "It's been my understanding that the doctors here will see you regardless of medical history."

"Interesting," I decided.

"There's something else," Alex hesitantly added.

My red flags went up. Was it me, or did the P.I. suddenly seem apprehensive? What didn't he want to tell me? If it was something pertinent to the case, then he'd damn well better cough it up.

"Hit me with your best shot," I groaned. "What do you have?"

"Perhaps I should show your two friends first," Alex began. "And then, if they approve, you would be allowed to watch it. I've been pestering the owner to give me this for quite some time. I can now say he finally sent me a copy."

"I would be allowed?" I incredulously repeated. "And a copy of what?"

"What do you have?" Vance asked.

Alex reached into his briefcase and pulled out a tablet computer. He tapped the screen to wake the device, entered in his access code, and then hesitated again. He tapped an icon on the screen and then slid the tablet over to Vance, who slowly picked it up.

"What am I watching?" Vance asked, puzzled. "Is there a reason you've ... oh. Oh, no."

"What?" I demanded. "What are you watching? Let me see it."

Vance held up a finger and encouraged me to wait. I studied my friend's face intently as I tried to figure out what he could possibly be watching. Then I watched his face drain of color and he suddenly flinched. He quickly shut the tablet off and gave it back to Alex. I started to reach for it when Vance smacked my hand away.

"No, Zack. Do not watch that. Trust me, buddy."

"Why? What is it?"

"Do you trust me?" Vance asked, as he turned to look at me.

"Yeah, I do. Why?"

"Then you need to listen to me now. Do not, and I repeat, do not watch this or make any attempts to watch it. That goes for you, too, Jillian."

"Can you tell me what it is?" I asked, even though I had a suspicion I knew what it was.

"It's dashcam footage from someone who was following your wife the day she died," Vance somberly reported. "He recorded the whole thing. Trust me, do not watch it."

For the second time that afternoon, I felt the blood drain from my face. Vance was right. The last thing I needed to see was the footage of my beloved Samantha being struck and killed. That would more than likely haunt me for the rest of my days.

I looked down at my hand. I had been reaching for the tablet, which, to his credit, Alex hadn't completely pulled away from me, but was keeping out of my reach. However, he hadn't placed it back in his briefcase yet, so he was prepared to give it to me, should I ask. I pulled my arm back, took a few deep breaths, and then nodded at Vance.

"All right, pal. You win. You're right. I don't want to see that. Now that you have, what can you tell me about it? And feel free to leave out the details."

"It was just as it had been described," Vance reported. "Her SUV was driving along fine, without showing any signs of mechanical duress. Then, out of the blue, it swerved to the left, down the median, and up into the oncoming lanes of traffic."

I shuddered, which had the result of Jillian clasping my hand tightly in hers.

"Are you okay?" Jillian quietly whispered.

It took a few moments, but I finally nodded.

"It never dawned on me that someone could have recorded the whole thing," I softly murmured. Sensing a growing queasiness in my stomach, I hastily took a few swallows of soda to help settle my nerves. "Was there anything else of note? Anything at all that could help us?"

Vance shook his head. "No, not that I could tell. Alex, could you send me a copy of that video? I'll go over it a few times more, just to see if there is anything that stands out."

"I can tell you I have gone over it quite a few

times," Alex admitted.

"And?" I prompted. "You noticed something, didn't you?"

"I noticed something suspicious, yes."

Vance reached for his pen.

"Go on. We're listening."

"You saw the video," Alex said, looking at Vance. "Did you notice those concrete dividers on the freeway?"

Vance shook his head. "No. What about them?"

"I reached out to the guy who shot that video, asking for more footage before the accident happened. He was able to provide the raw footage, which was nearly thirty minutes longer than the one you've seen. It confirmed my suspicions. There were concrete dividers the previous three miles, due to some type of construction."

"I remember hearing about the construction," I recalled.

"What about it?" Jillian asked. "How is that relevant?"

"It's relevant," Alex explained, "because as soon as the dividers stop, that was when the accident happened. Had she swerved five seconds before, the car would have hit the divider, and more than likely it probably would have just flipped over. As it was, without anything to stop the vehicle, it made it down the median and up to the other side."

"Didn't Harry suggest something like this earlier?" Jillian asked, as she turned to me. "We were all talking about road construction and why Sam's car would wait for the dividers to pass before veering off course. You thought it was suspicious then, and the more I hear about it, the more suspicious I become. This has to mean something, Zachary."

"It's a place to start," Vance admitted. He looked over at the PI and then longingly down at his briefcase. "I don't suppose I could prevail upon you to make me a copy of those files, do you? I'd love to be able to go over them tonight."

Alex reached into his briefcase and slid out a second manila folder. He passed them to Vance with a knowing grin on his face.

"I knew you were coming, Mr. Samuelson, and that you were a police detective. I had a copy waiting."

"You knew he'd want his own copy?" Jillian asked, incredulous.

Alex nodded. "Of course. He's a detective. I'd want the same thing if the roles were reversed."

After we finished our meal, we said our good-byes to the PI and headed back to our respective casitas. While Vance took the file back to his own room and reviewed Alex's notes, Jillian and I grabbed the leashes and took the dogs for a walk. The Phoenician must have some of the most beautifully landscaped grounds I think I have ever seen. Just south of the numerous pools was a narrow body of water that stretched from west to east, and nearly covered the full length of the resort. I later learned it was called Necklace Lake.

As we walked the dogs along the waterfront, I could feel beads of sweat start to trickle down my back. Yes, this was Phoenix, and yes, we were still in summer. But, for the record, I should mention it was the tail end of summer, which meant the days were starting to cool off and the nights were dipping down to normal temps. Yes, the temperature may be in the double digits, but it was still over 90 degrees in the shade, so I was starting to sweat. Concerned, I looked at Jillian, but I could see right off the bat she was enjoying the warmth. And the dogs? Both corgis, while outfitted in what I would have thought were heavy coats, were acting as though they were unaffected. In fact, I kept leaning down to pet their sides, just to make sure they weren't overheating. So far, so good, only I should point out that I caught both dogs staring longingly at the nearby lake, as if each wanted to go swimming.

"Think it's too warm out here for them?" I asked again.

"We're in the shade," Jillian reminded me. "We're essentially walking from one shaded area to the next, so they should be fine."

We had just reached the halfway point, where we found a white gazebo and a large circular fountain, when both dogs stopped in their tracks. Curious, I stopped, too, to see if I could tell what had attracted their attention.

"What is it?" Jillian asked, as she looked

around.

"I think the dogs smell something," I quietly told her. "They keep looking around, as if expecting something to appear."

Something did appear, and it was something that you wouldn't find in Oregon. It was a large, slender bird, measuring about 22 inches from beak to tail. The feathers were streaked white and dark brown, and the bird had a spiky crest on the top of its head. This fellow had three long tail feathers, each tipped with white, and the legs, I could see, had two toes in the front of the foot and two in the back. The bird cooed softly at me before switching to a loud repetitive clattering noise once it looked at the dogs.

"What is that?" Jillian wanted to know.

Proud that I knew the answer, I reared back and smiled. "That, my dear, is a roadrunner."

Surprised, Jillian looked back at the large bird and tilted her head, as though she wasn't sure that she believed me.

"I've seen the cartoons, Zachary. The roadrunner doesn't look anything like that."

I grinned. "Yeah, they left a few things out, that's for sure. You should have seen my reaction when I saw one for the first time. I was sitting at a picnic bench, eating a hamburger, when one of those things came right up to me."

"Are they that fearless?" Jillian asked, amazed.

"Well, they are a predator, that's for sure. I think many of them are used to receiving handouts. Anyway, this roadrunner came up to me, making that clacking noise you just heard. I figured he was hungry, so I broke off a piece of bread and tossed it down to him. Do you know what he did?'

"He ignored it," Jillian guessed.

"Right. I tossed a few more pieces down, being careful to avoid any condiments. He still ignored it. Then, out of sheer curiosity, I broke off a piece of the meat and tossed it to him. Man alive, he snapped that up like there was no tomorrow. They sure didn't show that in the cartoon. I always thought they ate seeds."

"Another childhood myth gone the way of the dodo," Jillian breathed.

The roadrunner ventured closer. Its loud clattering switched back to soft coos, like the sound a dove would make. Sherlock and Watson, both still frozen in place, watched the newcomer approach. Knowing full well that roadrunners were predators, and were known for killing lizards and rattlesnakes, and pretty much anything they were able to catch, I started pulling on the leashes. I wasn't going to risk either of the dogs getting hurt.

The roadrunner cooed again and took a few more rapid steps toward Sherlock, as though the corgi was offering the desert dweller a morsel of food. Sherlock, on the other hand, had started woofing softly at the intruder. His ears were straight up, his head cocked to the side, and one paw was frozen in mid-step.

As if uncertain whether or not the corgis were food, the roadrunner ventured closer still, and then stretched forward. Sherlock, thinking the strange bird was a weird type of dog and a proper canine introduction was required, stretched his neck forward so he could sniff noses with the bird. It was truly a Kodak moment, which had me reaching for my phone so I could snap a few pics. However, it wasn't meant to last. Heck, I don't think either dog or the bird were that impressed with the other, because the roadrunner's cooing switched back to the louder chattering, and he ran off. Oddly enough, the roadrunner had paused to look back at the dogs, as if expecting them to follow. It waited a full ten seconds before it finally ran off.

"Well, I don't know if you picked up another admirer or not," I told the dogs. "Come on. We've got work to do."

TWO

"T his has got to be one of the nicest resorts I've ever visited," Jillian was saying, as plates of food were set before us the following morning.

"What do you have there?" I curiously asked, as I studied her selection. "It looks like eggs on toast, but more importantly, what's that green stuff? Is that smooshed avocado? For breakfast?"

"It's avocado toast," Jillian confirmed. She took a small bite and a huge smile broke out on her face. She looked at me and cut off a small corner for me to sample. "Here. You need to try this."

"Avocado? For breakfast? I'm not sure about that."

"It's delicious. Try it. You'll like it, I'm sure."

I made sure Jillian wasn't watching and surreptitiously slid my glass of orange juice closer. I took the proffered sample and popped it in my mouth. Okay, it wasn't as bad as I thought, but I still wouldn't have chosen it for breakfast. I'm more of a cereal and toast type of guy when it comes to mornings. Or French Toast, which is exactly what I ordered.

Vance joined us moments later. He gently handed back the menu to the waitress and just ordered coffee. He studied Jillian's plate for a few moments before his surprised eyes found hers.

"Is that eggs and avocado? For breakfast? Huh."

"So," I started, between mouthfuls of the syrupy goodness that was my breakfast, "where should we start today?"

Vance drank some of his coffee and slid a piece of paper over to me. Both Jillian and I leaned forward to see what was written on it. It was a name and an address of someone who lived in Phoenix.

"Who's this?" I wanted to know, as I looked over at my detective friend.

"That's the guy who recorded the dashcam video of the accident. I want to talk to him."

"I'm sure he's already talked to the police," I assured him.

Vance was nodding, "Of that, I have no doubt. However, I want to get his feeling for the situation. What does he remember about the incident? Was there anything that stood out?"

"Do you really think he'll be able to remember anything new from an accident that happened nearly two years ago?" Jillian wanted to know.

Vance shrugged. "Honestly? I don't know. However, it's a place to start and it's worth a try."

"So, where does our witness live?" I asked, as we exited the restaurant and headed toward the van.

I was holding Sherlock's leash and Jillian had Watson's.

"You're still holding the paper the PI gave me," Vance pointed out. "You tell me."

"Oh." I pulled the paper from my pocket and checked the address. "Paradise Valley? Okay. That's a nice part of town."

"Where is it from here?" Vance wanted to know. "Is it far?"

"Not really," I reported. A quick glance at my watch confirmed that—thankfully—rush hour was over. "We should be able to make it there in about 20 minutes, provided traffic cooperates."

I lifted the dogs into the van, held Jillian's hand while she climbed in after them (which had Vance rolling his eyes at me) and slid the door closed.

"Suck-up," Vance muttered, as we pulled away. "Why do you do stuff like that? Are you trying to make me look bad?"

"Tori's not here," I reminded him. "What are you worried about?"

"I think it's chivalrous," Jillian told me, from her passenger seat behind me. "It's very romantic."

"Just don't do that type of thing around Tori, okay? You make me look bad."

"Well, you could really get on Tori's good side by opening doors for her and letting her enter first, or opening the car door for her, or..."

"I get it, I get it," Vance grumped. "I've been married for over thirteen years. I know how to keep my marriage going strong, thank you very much."

We headed west on Camelback Road until we hit 44th Street. Turning right, we were now angling north, and according to the signs, we were less than five miles from Paradise Valley. Alex Stokes' notes indicated the guy who shot the video of Sam's accident was a man by the name of Victor Aronson, and he lived behind Paradise Valley Community College.

Once again, I thanked my lucky stars that we didn't have to traverse the entire city to get to our destination. For the record, the Phoenix metropolitan region encompassed an area of 517 square miles. We could have easily been on opposite ends of the city from one another, and as a result, we could have spent close to an hour trying to find this guy's house. But, since we were both in the northeastern section of the city, we arrived in less than ten minutes.

Sam and I had been to Paradise Valley quite a few times. There were some fantastic restaurants in the area, and we usually came up here every other week. In fact, we just drove by one of our favorites, called the Salty Pig. They had some type of taco with slow-cooked pork belly that was to die for. In fact, we almost had an arm-wrestling contest right there in the restaurant to see who was going to lay claim to the leftovers.

I sighed as we drove by, a fact not lost on Jillian. She took my hand in hers and gave it an encouraging squeeze.

"Is everything okay?"

I hooked a thumb back the way we had come.

"We just passed one of Samantha's favorite restaurants. We ate there less than a week before she died. I haven't been back there since."

Vance glanced over at me and gave me a sympathetic look. "How are you doing with all of this, pal? I can't even begin to imagine how rough this must be. I don't think I'd be able to do it."

"It's not easy," I admitted, "but I'm all right. I have to deal with all of this sooner or later. Hey, there's the college. We must be getting close."

We arrived at the house five minutes later. The Aronson home was a typical southwestern style house with a flat roof and several faux posts jutting out along the roofline. And the color? A rich, adobe brown. As ugly as the color was, it worked for this particular house.

"Mr. Aronson? My name is Vance Samuelson. This is Jillian Cooper and over there with the two dogs is Zack Anderson. We spoke on the phone? I wanted to talk to you about the dashcam video of an accident on I-17 that you recorded almost two years ago ... late November. Do you remember the conversation?"

Mr. Aronson, a bald thirty-something black man who was covered with muscles and was wearing a yellow shirt and black jeans, slowly nodded. I watched Mr. Aronson give a slight cringe, which I could tell didn't go unnoticed by either Vance or Jillian. After a few moments, he held out a hand. Once the introductions were made, which included the dogs, we were ushered inside.

The house—in my opinion—was tastefully decorated. The living room had a high-end flat panel television and home theater setup, and for seating there was a full leather sectional with several built-in recliners. Both corgis bunched their legs, as though they were preparing to jump up onto the couch, when I cleared my throat and wagged a finger at them.

"You know the rules, guys. You're allowed on the furniture in our house only. Don't even think about it."

"It's okay," the homeowner assured us. "I like dogs."

"Thanks, Mr. Aronson," I told him, "but the dogs do know better. I think they're just seeing how much they can get away with."

"No worries. And call me Victor, please."

"Victor. Thanks."

Vance cleared his throat and pulled out his notebook. "Mr. Aronson? I ... sorry. I mean, Victor, do you remember the day I'm talking about? The one with the crash involving the blue Audi SUV."

This time, it was more pronounced. Victor shuddered again. His eyes closed and he had to give himself a full five seconds before he was able to continue. His dark eyes opened and he stared hard at Vance.

"What do you want to know about it?"

"I, er, take it you remember the accident?" Vance hesitantly asked.

Victor nodded. "Man, I will never, ever forget that day for as long as I live. Why do you want to know about that? I've been trying very hard to push that day out of my brain."

Vance looked over at me, as if to confirm I wanted him to continue. I held up my hand and signaled him to wait. Victor noticed the exchange and looked expectantly at me.

"As Vance mentioned before, my name is Zack Anderson. The reason we're asking about that particular accident is because, well, the driver of that SUV was my wife."

"Oh, shit," Victor muttered. "Would you excuse me for a moment?"

Victor Aronson left the room and disappeared through a doorway. I'm guessing it was the kitchen, because we suddenly heard the tell-tale sound of a cap being removed from a bottle. He returned, holding a beer. He looked at me, shook his head, and took a long swig from his beer.

"I'm sorry, Mr. Anderson."

"Call me Zack," I gently offered.

"Zack. I'm sorry. Would anyone else care for a beer?"

I glanced at my companions. Jillian's eyes were starting to fill. She blinked away her tears and nodded encouragingly at me. Vance was also nodding.

"Sure, Victor. That'd be great."

"Be right back."

Once we were all holding our beers, Victor encouraged us to take a seat on the couch. He drained his own beer and leaned back, allowing himself to sink lower into the cushions. After a few moments of uncomfortable silence, Victor began to speak.

"You guys have no idea what that day did to me. It's a day that will haunt me for the rest of my life."

"Can you tell us about it?" Jillian softly asked.

Victor nodded. "Yeah. I haven't really talked about it. Sheryl, my wife, has encouraged me to seek counseling, but I always made excuses not to go. Clearly, that was the wrong decision."

"Would you like me to get you another beer?" Jillian asked.

"Would you? The kitchen is right through there."

"Of course. I'll be right back."

Once Victor had taken a long pull from his second beer, he shook his head and started talking. His eyes, I noticed, never left the floor.

"I used to be a reckless driver," Victor began. His voice had become monotone, and devoid of emotion. "I'll be the first to admit it. People annoyed the hell out of me on the freeway. I always seemed to be in a hurry. That day, I remember being in a rush, like I always seemed to be in those days. I was zipping through traffic, getting angry at other drivers, and then got behind that Audi. Traffic slowed, so there was nowhere for me to go. I ended up following your wife, Zack, for what must've been a few miles. It was stop and go traffic, so you can imagine I had become so worked up that I was literally ready to blow a gasket. I was actually considering jumping onto the shoulder to pass all those slow-moving assholes that I ... oh. I'm terribly sorry, ma'am. I should have a care with my language."

Jillian waved off his concerns. "Trust me, I've heard a lot worse. From both of them. And from me, if you must know."

Victor briefly smiled. Then, his grin vanished as his eyes unfocused and he continued his narrative.

"I was about ready to downshift when it happened." Victor paused and took several deep breaths. "The Audi suddenly sped up and then swerved left, heading down the embankment. Thank God we were in the passing lane, because she would have hit whatever was next to us. As it was, there was nothing there but open space. Before I could even register what was happening, the Audi was up on the opposite side of the freeway, heading the wrong way. Damned if it didn't look like it was speeding up, too. I tried to warn her, man. I tried flashing my lights and blaring my horn, but nothing helped. Before I knew it, the Audi had slammed headfirst into a semi-truck. It ... uh, it burst into flames upon impact."

I suddenly discovered my mouth was dry. Bone dry. I swallowed a few times, to no avail. Remembering I was holding a beer, I quickly took a drink and waited for my tongue to recover, only it didn't. My hands felt clammy, and I was pretty sure I was close to hyper-ventilating. Jillian took my hand in hers and laced her fingers through mine.

"Zack? Zachary? Talk to me. Are you okay?"

I took a couple of deep breaths and waited a few moments to make sure my voice wouldn't fail me. Before I could say anything, both corgis whined with empathy and jumped up onto my lap. Sherlock's wet nose buried itself under my neck and he whined again. Watson curled up on my lap and steadfastly refused to leave.

"They're protecting him," Vance noted. "Anubis does that to Tori from time to time. Zack, are you okay?"

"I'm good," I assured my friend. "Keep going, Victor. Please."

"Ever since that day," Victor continued, "I haven't broken the speed limit. Not even by a little bit. I won't even change lanes without signaling first and then checking all blind spots at least twice. I'm tellin' you, man. That day has turned me into a little old lady driver. No offense, ma'am."

Jillian smiled at him. "None taken, Victor."

At that moment, there was a commotion at the door. A white woman, about the same age as Victor, wearing blue scrubs—which indicated she worked in some type of medical profession—with her blonde hair tied back in a ponytail, came through the door. She caught sight of the three of us and plastered a guarded look on her face. Then she saw the dogs in my lap and her expression turned into a frown. However, before she could say anything, Victor came to our rescue.

"Sheryl? This is Vance, Zack, and Jillian. The two dogs are Sherlock and Watson."

"Hello," the woman said, after a brief hesitation. "What's going on here? Are you friends of Victor's?"

Vance shook his head and was preparing an answer when Victor did it for him.

"Sheryl, Zack is the husband of the lady who was killed in that Audi."

Sheryl gasped with shock. She hurried over to Victor's side and took his hand in hers. She looked at me and her eyes filled with tears.

"Oh, I am so sorry for your loss. We didn't know your wife, but can honestly say no one deserved to die like that."

"Thanks," I quietly managed.

"Why are you here?" Sheryl suddenly asked. "Please don't tell me you're looking for copies of that blasted video. I refused to watch it. I saw what it did to Victor."

"I saw it," Vance announced, drawing everyone's attention to himself. "The P.I. gave me a copy. And, for the record, I wouldn't let Zack watch it."

"Good man," Victor quietly mumbled. "Wait, what? You hired a P.I.? Was that the guy who kept calling me? Why? To find me?"

I raised a hand. "It was me, Victor. I hired the P.I. I have reason to suspect my wife was murdered. To give you some context, the three of us all live in southwestern Oregon. My P.I., who's local to Phoenix, said I had to come down here. He said he found evidence Samantha's death was premeditated. Then he said he found dashcam footage of the accident."

"What about the footage?" Sheryl wanted to know. "Did he think there was something suspicious in it?"

Vance was nodding. "For the record, I noticed something that looked suspicious."

Everyone in the room, including the two corgis, I might add, turned to Vance. Sherlock, for his part, comically cocked his head, as though Vance was spewing gibberish. I gave him a good scratching behind the ears for that one.

"Before I answer that," Vance started, "am I right to understand that only the two of us have seen that video, Victor?"

Victor solemnly nodded.

"Okay. Did you notice the timing?"

"What timing?" Victor wanted to know.

"You told me you had been following the Audi for a mile or two. I couldn't quite tell in the video, but it looked like there was some type of construction going on, is that right?"

Sheryl nodded. "They added another northbound lane to I-17. What of it?"

"The concrete dividers!" Vance triumphantly exclaimed. He looked over at me and grinned.

"What about them?" Victor asked, confused. "I remember seeing them in the video. What of it?"

"Well, Harry called it," Vance continued. "At the exact instant those dividers stopped, the Audi veered left and headed straight over to oncoming traffic. Coincidence?"

Jillian and I glanced at Victor, whom I was relieved to say, had a puzzled expression on his face. After a few moments, he turned to his wife.

"Could you bring me my laptop, please?"

"You're not going to watch that video again, are you?" Sheryl angrily exclaimed. "I know what that thing did to you. I'd just as soon not go through it again."

"Baby, if that poor woman was killed on purpose, then I want to know. I want to help nail the bastards responsible. Please, would you bring me my laptop?"

Sheryl exited the room and returned moments later, holding a pencil-thin laptop. Victor set it on the coffee table, booted it up, and then started tapping the touchpad. The video began, complete with audio, when Victor suddenly paused it and looked over at me.

"You don't want to see this, do you? Here, I'll mute it. I don't need to hear that crash again, and Sheryl certainly doesn't need to hear me swearing like that. Okay, there's the Audi. Yes, I see those dividers. They're there, preventing anyone from crossing into the oncoming lanes."

"Is the freeway separated yet?" I asked, from my spot on the couch. I had still made no move to watch the video.

Vance sat up and moved over to sit on Victor's right side so he could see the video, too.

"Not yet, it isn't," Vance reported. "What speed do you think you were going there? I know it's not full speed, but then again, it's faster than your typical freeway crawl."

"Probably around 40," Victor answered. He fixed Vance with a neutral stare, and then noticed the small notebook in my friend's hand. "What do you do again, Vance?"

"Hmm? Oh, sorry. I'm a police detective up in Oregon."

"What part of Oregon?" Sheryl asked, innocently enough. "Did you say and I missed it?"

"Pomme Valley," Jillian answered. "It's in the southern part of the state. We're close to Grants Pass and Medford."

"Pomme Valley," Sheryl repeated softly. "Pomme Valley. Why is it I've heard of that town? Hmm. Would you excuse me for a moment?"

Victor's wife left the room and headed into the kitchen. Shrugging, Victor turned back to the video. He slapped a hand on the pause button moments before the Audi slammed into the truck. He shook his head, sighed, and looked over at me.

"I will admit that I never noticed it before. The Audi had ample time to swerve left, which would've ended up slamming into those dividers, but at least she wouldn't have made it the other side of the freeway. Of that, I'm sure."

"True," Vance admitted, "and I'm also certain she would've survived the crash. The rest of the traffic was moving too slow. They could have easily stopped in time."

Victor played the video over from the start and watched it a second time.

"I see what you mean, man. No wonder you're here, dude. If someone did that to Sheryl, I'd be doing the same damn thing you're doing: searching for answers. I..."

"Hang on a sec," Vance interrupted. He pointed at the screen. "Would you play that back, Victor? About 10 seconds, please."

"What are you looking for?" I asked, from my place on the couch. I still hadn't had the nerve to watch the video, and I doubted I would any time soon.

"It's something I noticed," Vance murmured quietly. "Something ... there. Did you see that? Play it again."

"It looks the same to me," Victor admitted.

"If I didn't know any better," Vance slowly began, as he watched the video progress in slow-motion, "then I'd say that she just stomped on the gas here. Did you see the Audi jerk? It looked like the front of the car lifted slightly, as if the driver were to slam their foot down on the accelerator."

"I think that was just because the road was

rough through there," Victor observed. "That's why the video shook."

"It was, yeah," Vance admitted, "but even with the screen shaking, you can see the Audi take off. Let it play forward. There, the Audi just took off down the median. Now it's in the oncoming traffic. Do you know what I didn't see?"

"What?" Jillian, Victor, and I all asked, together.

"Brake lights. Not once did she hit the brakes."

"What are you trying to say?" I demanded, growing angry. "That Samantha deliberately drove into oncoming traffic? I don't buy it."

"Nor do I," Jillian added.

"That goes for me, too," Vance admitted. "So, what does that tell us? That one of three things happened. First, as the police reports states, she could've lost control of the car and driven—unwillingly—into the opposing lanes of traffic."

"There's no way," Victor said, voicing his own concerns.

Vance nodded. "Right. That leads me to the second option: perhaps she suffered some type of medical trauma, which resulted in her losing control and going across the median."

I shook my head. "She didn't have any history of that happening."

"And third?" Jillian prompted.

"That her car was forced to hit that semi."

I frowned. "Forced? As in, forced off the road? Like someone ran her off the road? I would assume the footage failed to show that, or else you would have mentioned it by now."

"That's not what I'm saying," Vance argued. "All these new modern cars are now equipped with computerized controls. I'm suggesting someone might have hacked her car."

"What?" I demanded. "This isn't any movie. People don't do that type of thing."

Victor sat back in his chair, dumbfounded. He slowly nodded.

"I got a buddy who insists his Mercedes was hacked. Someone kept changing all his radio stations."

Sheryl returned just then, holding something that had my jaw dropping open with surprise. It was a bottle of Syrah, from a winery I was quite familiar with. Sheryl held the bottle out so that her husband could read the label.

"Do you see this, Victor? This wine that we just bought was bottled in Pomme Valley, Oregon. That's why the name was familiar to me."

"Lentari Cellars," I breathed, amazed.

It was Sheryl's turn to be surprised.

"You've heard of it? Really? Well, if you're from the same town, then I guess it's not that unusual."

I hesitantly raised a hand, like I was a nervous schoolboy ready to answer a question.

"The reason I know it is because that's my winery. I inherited it last year, after my wife died. That's why I moved. I needed a change of scenery."

Sheryl looked at me, thunderstruck. She held

the bottle out to me and waggled it in front of me.

"You're telling me that you are responsible for this? This bottle, right here?"

"I'm not, personally," I corrected. "My wine-master, Caden, handles all the recipes. But yeah, that bottle came from my winery. Honestly? I didn't know our wine was for sale outside of the state. Then again, that just proves to you how little I know about running the day to day operation of the winery."

"So, getting back on track," Jillian smoothly interjected, "is there any way of determining if Samantha's car was hijacked? And, if so, could someone take over the controls and tell it where to go?"

Vance pulled out his cell and looked at me. "What was the model of her car again?"

"It was a 2017 Audi Q7," I automatically answered. "It was her dream car."

Vance tapped his search into his smartphone and then perused the results. He suddenly grunted, tapped the screen once, and grunted again. Curiosity piqued, I leaned forward.

"What is it? What did you find?"

"That particular model has Driver Assist."

"Yeah, I remember that. It was to help her parallel park. She hated parallel parking."

"Who doesn't?" Sheryl quipped, eliciting a grin from her husband.

"So it helps with parking," I said, "so what? It's not like it was a self-driving car, so that really doesn't help us too much."

Vance waggled his phone. "Nevertheless, I think we ought to talk to an Audi mechanic and get their take on this. I'd like to know if it's possible."

"How terrifying would that be?" Jillian whispered. "To know that the car you're driving could be taken over? That makes me want to go back to riding my bicycle."

"You and me both," I agreed.

Vance stood, which prompted Jillian and me to do the same. My detective friend held out a hand.

"Thank you, Victor. You've been a tremendous help. Sheryl, it was nice to meet the two of you."

"If you don't mind me asking," Sheryl hesitantly began, "what's next for you? Do you really think someone set up that poor woman to be killed?"

I nodded affirmatively. "That's the theory at the moment. The more I look into this, the more convinced I become."

"I hope you find the sumbitch who did this to your wife," Victor solemnly told me. "If there's anything I can do, then you are to let me know. Knowing I helped bring her killer to justice might just make the nightmares stop."

I shook Victor's hand. "I'll keep you posted, pal. Thanks again for your hospitality. Sheryl? Victor? I'll personally send a case of the Syrah for you two, as a way of saying thanks."

"Dude, there's no need to ... oomph!" Victor

was cut off after Sheryl thumped him in the gut. "I mean, that'd be more than generous of you," he hastily amended.

I grinned. "Spoken like a true married man."

THREE

O h, I haven't been to one of these in a while. Come on, we gotta pull over."

"Zack, what am I looking at?"

"Seriously? Vance, you're looking at a modern southwestern marvel. The convenience stores around here are absolute wonders to behold. This one is called a 'PS'. We can get something to drink and a bite to eat, like a hot pretzel, if you want."

"We're going to a place called BS and you want to get a drink? What, is this a joke? It looks like a gas station to me."

"P," I corrected. "PS, not BS. Big difference."

Jillian tapped Vance on the shoulder and pointed at the large sign, depicting only two letters: PS.

"Oh. So, it *is* a gas station. You want to get food here? Come on, pal. You can do better than that. If you're hungry, then I'm sure we can find a decent place to grab a bite."

It was too warm to leave the dogs in the car without the air conditioning running, so Jillian volunteered to wait with them. Her only request was for me to pick her up a cherry Pepsi. As Vance and I walked through the store, I pointed out all the offerings that were available. My detective friend's objection to getting a bite to eat was quickly withdrawn as he started tapping the touchscreen menu, which listed all the choices that were available. He was in the process of ordering a pizza when I felt a light tap on my shoulder. Turning, I came face-to-face with someone I was not expecting to see.

"Zack? Oh, man! I thought that was you! Holy cow, brother! I didn't know you were back in town!"

The owner of the voice was nearly fifteen years younger than I was, had unkempt blonde hair, and had to be a full ten inches shorter than me. This was a person I had known for practically all his life, and I'm sad to say, I hadn't spoken a word to him since the day Samantha died. Who was it, you ask? Well, his name was Randy. *Is* Randy. Randall Masters, if you want to get technical. He was Samantha's much younger little brother.

"I'll be damned. Hey, Randy. How are you?"

"Dude, what the hell are you doing here? Didn't you move out of state?"

"To Oregon," I confirmed. "Listen, I know I should have stopped by and talked to you guys, but..."

Randy nodded knowingly and brushed off my concerns, "Dude, what you went through was thoroughly messed up. I wouldn't wish it on my worst enemy. I may have lost a sister, but you lost your wife. Mom always told me that you knew her better than anyone, including her. We all knew it was rough on you. So, what are you doing back in town? Will you be here for a few days?"

Hoo, boy. Where do I start? Do I admit the real reason we were here?

"Is this a friend of yours?" Vance's voice suddenly asked, as he appeared by my side.

I nodded. "It is. Vance, this is Randy, Samantha's brother. Randy, this is a friend of mine, from Oregon. He's here, helping me to check out a few things."

Randy's brow furrowed. "Oh? Like what?"

I wasn't too sure how Randy was going to take the news of me investigating his sister's death. Obviously, anything I tell him now will make it back to his parents, so I wasn't sure I should tell him we were treating his sister's death as a homicide. With that being said, I did feel that Samantha's family were part of my own extended family, so maybe I shouldn't keep any secrets from them.

An idea formed as I remembered the line of work that Randall and his father were in, and it had me smiling.

"Randy, are your parents home? I think I would like to stop by and say hello."

Randy checked his watch, "Well, I know Dad does a lot of his work from home, so he should be there. As for Mom, I think her shift ended at 10 a.m., which was just under an hour ago. So, yeah, they should both be there."

I should point out that Samantha's father, Jason Masters, owned and operated an insurance investigative firm, which meant he's done lots of research in his day. Randall Masters worked for his dad, as an estimator. As for Denise, Samantha's mother, she was a nurse.

"You're up to something," Randy accused, growing serious. "Can't you tell me what you're doing?"

I nodded. "I will, pal, but I want to tell your family at the same time. You all deserve to know."

"Deserve to know what?" Randy wanted to know.

"Nuh uh. I'll tell you all together."

We completed our purchases and headed outside. Randy followed us to our van and, once he saw who was waiting for us inside, turned to give me a speculative look. Thankfully, before an awkward silence could cut in, Randy gave me a friendly slap on the back.

"Good for you, bro. I'm really glad to see you're moving on. Did you want to follow me to my parents' house? They ended up moving since, uh, well, since Sam's death."

I nodded. "Sure. Sounds good."

"In case we get separated, they're off of 12th and Fern Drive now. It's not far from here."

Randy proceeded to hop into a blue Mustang convertible and speed off. It's a damn good thing he told us roughly where it was, because when it came to driving, Randy has always had a lead foot. And, he was no different now. Since our minivan could go from 0-60 in about an hour and a half, we were understandably left in his dust.

As I plugged in the intersection of 12th and Fern Drive into my phone, both dogs suddenly perked up. They each took a window and looked out at the businesses and stores that were passing by. Sherlock woofed again.

"What are you looking at, boy?" I asked, as I tried to determine where Sherlock was looking.

"What's out there?" Vance wanted to know.

I shrugged. "Not much. I see a little mini mall. There are a few stores in it, including a Square L convenience store. We both know how Sherlock reacts whenever he sees one of those."

Sherlock had a habit of suspiciously staring at that particular chain of convenience stores whenever we passed one by. Why? I can only imagine it had something to do with finding a certain Egyptian pendant, and all the praise that came with it, when I realized Vance had lost his bet. Consequently, the bet was whether or not he'd have to take tap dancing lessons while wearing his old Peter Pan outfit. So, if you're curious, just look up 'Detective dresses like Peter Pan' on YouTube and you can see for yourself.

Sherlock continued to woof for another five seconds before settling back down on the floor. What he was looking at, I don't know. I may never know.

"There's his car," Jillian pointed out, as we turned onto Fern Drive. "That must be their house right over there."

Randy must have phoned ahead, because a woman with bright red hair and a tall man with a solid head of gray hair were pacing in their driveway. Samantha's mother was still in her nurse's scrubs, and her father was wearing a gray Polo shirt and khaki pants, looking as immaculate as I remembered him. As our van pulled in, both of Samantha's parents immediately angled toward the driver side. However, they caught sight of Vance, who gave them each a sheepish smile, and immediately switched their attention to the passenger side.

"Zachary!" Denise Masters exclaimed, pulling me into a hug as soon as I stepped out. "It's so good to see you!"

Samantha's father caught my hand and crushed it in a bone-shattering handshake, "It's good to see you, son. You can imagine our surprise when Randy called to let us know who he had bumped into at the gas station."

"What's going on?" Denise worriedly asked, as she caught sight of the guarded expression on my face.

"First, let me introduce you to everyone. Vance? Jillian? These are the Masters, Samantha's family. That's Denise and this is Jason. Jillian? Over there is Randy, Samantha's brother. Guys?

This is Vance, a good friend of mine, and this is Jillian, my new girlfriend. They're both from Oregon and they're both here to help me with something."

"What part of Oregon did you end up moving to?" Jason wanted to know. "And they're here to help you with what?"

"Pomme Valley," I answered. "And I'll get to the other question in just a bit. As for PV, it's in the southwestern part of the state. Oh, before we go any farther, I have two more introductions to make." I turned back to the van and retrieved Sherlock first, and then Watson. I handed Watson's leash to Jillian as I turned around. "It's a long story, but I ended up adopting two dogs once I moved to Oregon. This is Sherlock, and that's Watson."

"Sherlock and Watson," Denise cooed. "How adorable! They're corgis, aren't they? Did you name them yourself?"

I pointed at Sherlock. "He was already named when I got him. As for Watson, well, I named her to go along with his name."

"Watson is a girl?" Randy asked, puzzled. "That's no name for a girl dog."

A smug smile appeared on Vance's face, to which, in response, I punched him on his arm before he could say anything. Then I saw Denise focus her attention on Jillian. I held my breath as I realized I had failed to take into consideration how Samantha's family would react to learning about my new relationship. For the second time,

I was surprised there wasn't an awkward silence, because Denise looked straight at me and smiled warmly.

"It's so good to see you moving on, Zack. Jason and I were worried about you. Let's go inside, shall we? Then you can tell us why you're here."

"How do you know there's a reason?" I asked.

"Because I know how hard this must be for you to come back here, and especially to see us. Plus, Randy indicated you needed to talk to us, so either you're going to announce your intent to marry Jillian..."

Jillian and I quickly looked at each other before turning away. I'm sure I blushed as red as a Coke can, while Jillian nervously giggled. Denise smiled at the two of us again before continuing on.

"... or, there's something more important on your mind. So, let's go inside, where we'll be more comfortable."

Once inside, with the three of us sitting together on a huge sectional, and the dogs were curled up by my feet, I looked at our hosts and took a deep breath. What I had to say was not going to go over well, that much was for sure. How, then, do I bring it up?

"What's going on, son?" Jason quietly, but firmly, asked. "What do you need to tell us?"

I immediately rose to my feet and began to pace. Sherlock rose to his feet, intent on following me, when I signaled he should remain in place.

"I've got something to tell you guys, and I'm

not sure how you're going to take it."

"Is this about Samantha?" Randy asked.

I nodded. I kept pacing a few moments longer before I finally stopped. I looked over at Jason, father of my beloved Samantha, and squatted down next to him.

"I'm here, well, we are here, because I believe Samantha's accident wasn't an accident."

Jason stood so fast that he bumped into me, which caused me to go tumbling backwards. Not being fans of sudden movement, both dogs leapt to their feet and stared at Jason, who at the moment, was clenching his fists uncontrollably.

"Why do you say that?" Denise somberly asked. Was it me, or had an edge of annoyance crept into her voice? "The police looked into the matter after it happened. They didn't find anything out of the ordinary. Zachary, you must know how badly Samantha's death had affected us all. It took a lot of counseling for us to come to terms with this. I'm really not sure I want to open up those wounds again."

I slowly rose to my feet. I looked at Denise and sighed as I reclaimed my spot on the couch.

"And, if you knew that someone was responsible for making the accident happen, wouldn't you want to know?"

"I would want to know the name of the person responsible," Jason flatly stated.

Why, all of a sudden, did I get the impression that, if I happened to know who was responsible, and I disclosed that name to Samantha's father, then I'd be signing that person's death warrant? There was just something about the way he stated his intentions. There was a dangerous glint in Jason's eyes. I definitely need to be careful what I share with him.

"For the past year," I slowly began, "I've been receiving phone calls at 3:30 in the morning practically every single day of the week. There was never anyone there, nor did I ever get any inclination who it was. That, however, came to a screeching halt a little over three months ago, when a female voice appeared on the line and claimed she was a friend of Samantha's. She then claimed she and Sam were coworkers."

You could have heard a pin drop in the Masters' household at that moment.

"She told me that Sam's death wasn't an accident. She told me that was why she had been calling me every morning at 3:30 a.m."

"Did she say what her name was?" Denise asked.

I shook my head. "No."

"You learned this over two months ago?" Jason asked, dumbfounded. "Why didn't you reach out to us, son? We could've helped! I'll dedicate every waking moment to helping you, if what you say is true."

I held up a finger. "Just wait. There's more."

Jason, who was preparing to fire off another angry outburst, hastily closed his mouth and settled back onto the couch.

"After that day, I contacted Vance here, and asked him to reopen Sam's case."

Both of Samantha's parents turned to regard Vance, as if they were seeing him for the first time.

"I'm sorry, I should have mentioned he is a police detective in Pomme Valley. He agreed to look at the file for me."

"You're lucky," Randy breathed, drawing everyone's attention over to where he had been quietly sitting. "How many people can say they're friends with an actual detective?"

"We met the day Zack moved to PV," Vance casually remarked. "It was the day I arrested you for murder, wasn't that right, Zack?"

Both Denise and Jason gasped loudly with surprise while Randy's eyes widened with shock.

"That's ancient history, pal," I grumbled. "And thank you so very much for bringing that up at this moment."

"You were convicted of murder?" Denise asked.

"Vance said he was accused, not convicted," Jason reminded his wife. "There's a big difference there."

"I was set up," I clarified. Then I pointed down at Sherlock. "Believe it or not, he's the main reason why I didn't land in jail. Sherlock and Watson both have a nose for finding clues that, to the outside observer, would appear pointless. However, every darn time these two stop to look at something, it's revealed to be relevant to the case."

Everyone present in the room studied the two

corgis. Sherlock, for his part, gazed back at everyone staring at him, as if to say, yep, you heard that right. I gave both dogs a pat on their heads.

"If you want the honest truth," Vance suddenly chimed in, "then you ought to know that those two dogs are responsible for solving, what are they up to now, Zack? Six murders?"

Jason stared incredulously at the two corgis.

"They've solved six murders? I'll be damned. Oh. That's why they're here, aren't they? You think they might be able to help you solve Samantha's death?"

I nodded encouragingly at Jason. "That's precisely why they're here. Once my P.I. said I needed to..."

"You hired a P.I.?" Randy interrupted. "For true?"

I nodded again. "I hired a local guy to look into the matter after that day with the phone call."

"What did he find?" Jason anxiously asked. "He had to have found something, because that's clearly why you're here. Please tell us. Let me know what I can do to help."

"There is something I think you might be able to do for me," I told Jason.

"There is?" Vance asked.

"There is?" Jason echoed. "Consider it done. What can I do for you?'

"First," I said, as I held up a finger, "I'll tell you that the P.I. found dashcam footage of the accident. Before you ask, no, I'm not going to show it

56

to you. Vance has seen it, and has steadfastly refused to let me see it. Based on that alone, I will not let you see footage of Samantha's accident."

"Thank you," Denise whispered.

I glanced over at Randy and noticed his face had turned ashen. Then I noticed Jason, and the firm look of resolve that had come over his features. I waggled my finger at him.

"No. I can see it in your eyes. You want to see the video. Trust me, you don't."

"He's not wrong," Vance added. "You should also know that we talked to the person who recorded the video earlier today."

Jason was taken aback. "Oh?"

"That was someone who definitely needs some counseling," Jillian added. "Even he admitted he needed to go. He told us that he hasn't been the same behind a wheel ever since it happened."

Jason's resolve crumbled. I saw his lips tremble and his eyes filled. Before I could offer any words of encouragement, he turned away and disappeared down a hallway. We heard the telltale signs of someone blowing their nose. Moments later, he was back. His eyes were clear and his composure was back.

"Was there anything on the video which caught your P.I.'s eye?" Sam's father finally asked.

"There was something that definitely caught mine," Vance said.

My detective friend then spent the next ten minutes giving the Masters family a recap of what had happened during our visit with Victor. My late wife's family sat there in silence as they digested this piece of news.

"And apparently Sam didn't hit the brakes once," I softly added.

"What?" Jason demanded. "That's not possible. Samantha was a perfect driver."

"And that's where you come in," I said, as I looked at Jason. "This is where I'm hoping you can help me out."

Jason nodded. "Of course. What can I do?"

"You still have your insurance investigation firm, right?"

Jason nodded again. "Yes. I'm starting to wind things down as I prepare to retire, but I still take cases from time to time from all the big name insurance companies. How would that help you?"

"I'm guessing you have contacts in the automotive industry?"

Jason nodded.

"Would you please find out if it's possible to hack a 2017 Audi Q7 and make it veer off course? I know that particular model has something called Driver Assist, which was supposed to help the driver parallel park, but I want to know if it's possible for someone to remotely take control of her car."

Jason was silent as he considered the request. I could see his lips moving as he softly started mumbling. He wordlessly rose to his feet, retrieved a spiral notebook from another part of the house, and returned to the couch. In moments, he was busy jotting down some notes.

"Is there something I can do?" Randy asked. "I'd like to help, too."

I looked over at Vance, who shrugged helplessly.

"Tell you what, Randy," I began. "If there's anything else I need while we're here in Phoenix, I'll let you know, okay? Give me your cell number and I'll give you mine."

Once everyone had exchanged numbers, and the overall atmosphere had lightened considerably, I finally felt like I could relax. Somewhat.

"How's your writing coming along?" Denise asked, ten minutes later, as she sipped on a bottle of water and passed a bottle to each of us. "Have you published any new novels?"

I nodded. "A few. And, I'm proud to say, they're tearing up the charts, so I cannot complain."

"Proof positive that there are a lot of romance readers out there," Vance joked.

Mortified, I glared at Vance. Samantha's family knew I was a writer, and that I had written a few science-fiction books years ago, but they did not know about my romance titles. Vance offered an apologetic smile and whipped out his notebook, as though it was imperative that he had to immediately check his notes.

"You can relax, Zachary," Denise told me. "We know all about Chastity Wadsworth and her many exploits."

Vance sniggered, Jillian giggled, and I choked on my water. I stared, flabbergasted, at Denise before I turned to look at Jason. Samantha's father, to his credit, didn't smile, but he did wink at me, which as far as I was concerned, made it worse.

"You knew?" I asked. "You all knew? How? When? Samantha said she never told you anything."

"She didn't," Denise confirmed. "But, she did show up here one day with a copy of your very first romance novel. She left it here by mistake..."

"Mistake, my eye," I grumbled.

"...and I couldn't help but read it. It was quite good! So, when I noticed other books being released by the same author, I picked them up as well. Do you see the bookcase over there? You'll find a copy of every book you've ever published. We are very proud of you, Zachary. My heavens, what an imagination you have."

Once again, I felt my face flame up. In fact, I know it did, 'cause I heard Jillian giggling uncontrollably.

"It sounds to me, pal," Vance began, trying valiantly to keep from laughing, "like you suck at keeping secrets."

"Do you remember a relative by the name of Abigail Lawson?" I suddenly asked. I was curious to see which side of the family she hailed from. I was guessing it was Jason's.

Both Denise and Jason nodded.

"Yes. She's a distant cousin," Jason told me.

"Second or third cousins, I believe. Why do you ask?"

"Have you ever met her?" I wanted to know.

Both Jillian and Vance had fallen completely silent.

Jason shook his head. "No, I haven't. What about you, honey?"

Denise also shook her head. "I have only heard the name in passing reference. I've never met that branch of my father's family tree."

Mother's side. Damn. I guessed wrong.

"Why do you ask?" Jason wanted to know.

"Well, I had originally thought she was the one who was calling every morning, bright and early. However, I now know it wasn't her."

"She and Zack don't really get along," Vance confirmed.

"Why's that?" Jason asked. "I take it you've met her?"

"It turns out that side of your father's family has links to Pomme Valley. Abigail's mother, one Bonnie Davis, left her house and winery to me. Well, to the two of us, but since Sam was out of the picture, it fell to me."

"You inherited a winery?" Denise asked, amazed. "If memory serves, you have never enjoyed wine. How ironic!"

"It's true," I shrugged. "I still don't. Anyway, Abigail felt cheated out of her inheritance and started pestering me to sign over the house and the winery to her."

"I sure as hell hope you told her where she could stick it," Randy vehemently declared.

"Randall!" Denise scolded. "You watch your language!"

"I'm thirty-one, Mom. I'm not a kid anymore."

"She means, watch your language whenever women are present," Jason coolly translated.

Randy looked at Jillian and sheepishly smiled. "Sorry, Jillian."

"I was referring to your mother," Jason said, "but she'll do, too."

I leaned forward to rest my elbows on my knees.

"Did you know that she has tried to force me to sign over the property on more than one occasion? She even claimed she had investors in her pocket and wanted to purchase the winery and move it out of Oregon. You see, the reason I'm telling you this is because I came across some old letters, correspondence between Abigail and her mother, and one thing became perfectly clear: Bonnie had no desire to sell her winery."

"I can't say that I blame her," Jason agreed. "When you put your heart and soul into something, and make it great, then the last thing you want to see is it sold off to the highest bidder."

I nodded. "Exactly. So, in honor of Bonnie's generosity, and for Samantha's side of the family, I kept the winery and reopened it."

"What's the winery called?" Denise wanted to know.

"Lentari Cellars," Jillian answered. "They make the absolute best Syrah. I believe Caden is up to four different recipes now, isn't he?"

"He added that special dessert wine," I reminded her. "The one that actually doesn't taste so bad."

"It doesn't taste so bad because it's a sweet wine," Jillian recalled. She looked at Samantha's family and smiled. "As you probably know, Zachary has the biggest sweet tooth I have ever seen on a person."

Denise nodded knowingly. "Oh, that's old news, dear. Do you want to get on his good side? Make him a plate of homemade chocolate chip cookies. You can get him to do just about anything for fresh cookies."

I shrugged. "Guilty as charged." I rose to my feet, which prompted the others to follow suit. "We've taken up enough of your time. It's been great seeing you guys again. Thanks for the understanding and support."

"We'll be in touch," Jason promised. "I'll get working on that request of yours."

"And don't forget to let me know if there's something I can do to help," Randy added.

"I will," I assured him.

"Where are you off to next?" Denise asked.

I looked down at the dogs, who were now both pulling on their leashes. They knew it was time to go and were ready for their next car ride.

"I think we're going to start doing some digging

on Semzar Pharmaceuticals. I need to find a way to get Sherlock and Watson to meet the people there. Then, if they zero in on anyone, we'll have something to work with."

I noticed Randy pull his cell phone out and begin tapping the screen. We had just said our goodbyes and had stepped outside when he came rushing out to us.

"You're in luck, Zack. Semzar Pharmaceuticals is currently holding some type of retreat at a local Phoenix hotel. It says tomorrow will be the last day."

"The last day for what?" I wanted to know. "And how do you know this?"

Randy held up his phone, "I'm reading it right from their own website. Let's see. They're calling this a company-wide team building event. I don't even know what that means."

"Neither do I," I had to admit. "But, that'll be perfect. It's at a hotel? Does it say which one?"

"It's at some Hilton that's fairly close to their office building. According to Semzar's website, they've booked all the conference rooms until 4 p.m. Looks like that's when they're finished."

"Perfect," I said, pleased. I shook Randy's hand. "See? You wanted to help, well, congrats! You just did."

"Sweet. Let me know if there's anything else I can do."

"That goes for me, too," Denise quietly added.

I faced Samantha's family and smiled at them.

"Thanks guys. I definitely will. It means a lot."

"The next time we go shopping for wine, we'll have to look for your label," Jason announced. "I'd certainly like to give your wine a try."

"It's for sale somewhere around here," Jillian announced. "The man who recorded the dashcam footage actually had a bottle in his house. We were all floored."

"I'll find it," Jason vowed. "Good luck!"

FOUR

D o you really expect us to twiddle our thumbs in here for the entire day?" Vance asked, as he frowned at me. "We've been sitting here for several hours now, and neither of the dogs has so much as lifted their heads. In fact, they look as bored as I feel."

We were sitting in the lobby of the only Hilton property I could find that was large enough to accommodate a retreat for a client the size of Semzar Pharmaceuticals. Plus, there was a sign just inside the lobby, which stated that the Hilton welcomes Semzar employees and hoped that their stay was a pleasant one. Just around the corner from the main entrance, and sitting directly opposite the check-in counter, was a comfortable seating area with four plush chairs. The three of us were relaxing in the chairs and chatting about which new *Star Wars* movie outshone all the others. Sherlock and Watson were curled up by my feet, and kept trying to snooze away the hours. Every time a person walked by, whether a member of the hotel staff or else someone that had to be from Semzar, I would give each of the dogs a slight nudge and make sure they were awake. So far, as Vance had pointed out, we had been sitting here since just after 9 a.m. with nothing to show for it.

My stomach rumbled then, reminding me that lunchtime was just around the corner. Jillian looked up from her magazine and smiled.

"Was that your stomach? We should probably get something to eat."

Vance perked up. "From where? Is there a restaurant nearby?"

"Is right around the corner close enough?" I asked with a smile. "This hotel has its own restaurant on the ground floor. That's why I'm getting hungry. They're cooking something, and it smells fantastic."

"There is also a food truck outside," Jillian reminded me. "I saw them when I took Watson out to go potty nearly half an hour ago. I think they were selling Mexican food."

"Oooo, that sounds good," Vance grinned, as he rubbed his hands together.

I shook my head. "I thought it sold Chinese food."

Vance shrugged and stood up. "Mexican, Chinese, I personally don't care. I'll have whatever is out there."

"What about the restaurant here in this hotel?" Jillian asked.

Vance shook his head. "I'll go there only if I can't find anything good outside. In fact, you two stay here. I'll go out to see whose memory is the best."

While Vance was gone, no doubt confirming that the food truck was selling Mexican food, a group of people suddenly walked through the hotel's main entrance. There were four guys and two women, and all of whom, I might add, were dressed in business attire. The four guys were wearing immaculate suits, while the two women wore blazers and skirts. None of them looked to be over forty.

As the group passed us, every single one of them noticed the corgis and made a comment or two about how cute the dogs looked, especially since Sherlock raised his head and watched them walk by. I also might add that he had started woofing.

"What do we do now?" Jillian excitedly whispered. "If Sherlock has taken notice, then wouldn't that mean one—or all of them—are worth investigating?"

I hastily pulled out my cell and began taking pictures as fast as I could. However, all I really accomplished was taking some quite tasteful butt shots of all of them. Damn! Vance is going to give me hell for missing the opportunity to get some photographic evidence we could use later.

Apparently, the powers above deemed me worthy for a second chance because all of a sudden, the business-clad group of six appeared again in the lobby. This time, it looked as though they were angling for a tiny convenience store selling water, candy, and various other sundries. As the group made their selections, I noticed the two women were eyeing the corgis, as though they'd like to come over and say hello but were afraid to get dog hair on their clothes.

Whatever.

This time, both Jillian and I pretended to be engrossed with our phones, but we were instead covertly taking snapshots of the group as they walked by us for a third time. One of the women, the last to make a purchase at the tiny shop, and therefore the last to walk by us on their way out, held out her bag as she walked by. Uncertain of her intentions, I hesitated, only to have the bag thrust into my hands as she passed, all without breaking stride. Then she hurried to catch up to her companions, all without bothering to look behind her to see what I was doing with her bag.

"What was that all about?" Jillian asked, confused. "Do you know that woman, Zachary?"

I shook my head. "Nope. I've never seen her before in my life."

Jillian pointed at the bag. "Why did she give you that? What's in it?"

I pulled out a Snickers candy bar and stared at it, as though it was an alien artifact that had been smuggled out of Area 51.

"A Snickers? She bought you a Snickers? What

in the world for?"

"I really don't know," I confessed. When I went to drop the candy back into the bag, the receipt caught my eye. Something had been scribbled on the back, with a blue pen:

GLAD YOU'RE HERE. CAN'T TALK NOW, BEING WATCHED. HAVE SOMETHING YOU'LL WANT. WILL CALL USUAL TIME.

"And you're sure you don't know her?" Jillian insisted.

"I swear, I've never seen her before in my life."

"Never seen who before?" Vance wanted to know, as he slid back into his seat. He was holding several white paper bags, each of which had some enticing aromas emanating from within. "You lost, Zack. It was Mexican food."

"I gathered that from the smell. Oh, well. I won't complain, seeing how whatever you have there smells great. Hey, did you see that group of six people come walking in here about five minutes ago?"

Vance nodded. "Four guys and two girls?"

"That's the one. Well, one of the women just handed me this bag and didn't say a damn thing about it."

Vance took the bag and looked in. His eyes lit up when he saw the Snickers.

"Hey, my favorite. Do you mind?"

"Go ahead," I encouraged my friend. "But, before you do anything, check out the receipt."

Vance pulled the receipt out, smoothed it, and then noticed the writing on the reverse side. As soon as he flipped it over, he let out of grunt of surprise.

"By any chance, did either of you get her picture?"

"We were too slow on the first attempt," Jillian informed him. "As soon as the dogs started woofing, we were pulling out our phones, only they had already walked by us."

"We got some great shots of their butts," I added, with a grin.

Vance groaned aloud, "That's not gonna help us, buddy."

"I know that. The rest of that story is they came back to buy some stuff at that little store there. That's when we took some pictures. But, as they all walked by us again, the lady bringing up the rear shoves this bag into my hands and then hurries off."

"Zack, how can you be so slow!" Vance moaned.

"Hey!" I snapped, growing angry. "There's no need to be snarky!"

"Zack, don't you get it? That woman must be your mystery caller. The note says that she's glad to see you. It even says she'll call you at the normal time. That's 3:30 in the morning, right? Er, make that tomorrow morning? And didn't you say that your mystery lady was your late wife's co-worker?"

Oh. Okay, maybe I was a dummy for not piecing

it together sooner. Sure, there was a chance this woman made a mistake and thought I was someone else, but more than likely, Vance will be right. She was evidently the source of my morning wake-up call for nearly a year.

I eagerly pulled my phone back out and perused through the pictures.

"Which one is she?" Vance asked, coming up to stare at my phone over my shoulder.

"This one," I said, as I zoomed in on the red-headed woman's face.

The woman in question looked to be in her late thirties, had crow's feet around her eyes, which I thought was unusual since she appeared to be too young to have wrinkles, and bore a worried look on her face. I checked all the pictures I had taken of her, including Jillian's as well, and noticed that not once had she bothered to look my way.

"What do you think she has that you want?" Vance asked, breaking the silence. "Any ideas?"

I shook my head. "None whatsoever. I might not have been the best with faces, but I think I would have remembered meeting a friend of Sam's."

"What are you saying?" Jillian asked. "Do you think she's making up the part about being Samantha's co-worker?"

"I can't imagine why she'd lie about that," I said.

Just as we were pulling the lunch Vance had procured for us out of the bags, a group of nearly forty similarly clad people, men and women alike, walked by us. They were merrily chatting among themselves and paid little attention to us. Sherlock and Watson, on the other hand, were on their feet and watching the procession. Almost immediately, Sherlock began his soft woofing. Watson didn't bark, whine, or woof at any of them, although I could tell she was softly growling.

The three of us must've looked like the Three Stooges. Burritos, tacos, and chimichangas went flying as we all abandoned our food and tried to nonchalantly pull out our phones and snap a few pictures. The woman who had given me the Snickers and the receipt with the message was also there, only as before, she didn't make eye contact.

She had said she was being watched. If this was Samantha's co-worker, and was the one who was making insinuations that my wife's death hadn't been an accident, then maybe she was in some type of danger. Maybe she couldn't stop to chat without giving herself away to the company's bigwigs.

The large group of Semzar employees, which consisted of both men and women, headed outside. Within moments, all forty of them had disappeared around the corner. However, I knew they had to be close, or else moving slow, because I could still hear them. I looked over at Vance, shrugged helplessly, and gathered up the dogs' leashes. In a matter of moments, we were in pursuit.

"Where are they going?" Jillian asked me, once she and Vance had caught up to us.

I pointed at an area just to the left of where the mass of people seemed to be heading.

"Just over there is a large grassy area. There are trees, a few tables, and there's even a small pond. As for what they're doing, I have no idea. I couldn't even tell you what 'team building' even means."

Jillian was thoughtful as she considered.

"If I were to venture a guess, then I'd say they are going to do some type of exercise where they'll probably be forced to rely on their companions in order to accomplish it. You know, in an attempt to build up the trust that exists between people?"

"Do people really do those sorts of things in a corporate environment like this?" Vance asked. "I mean, what benefit could it possibly provide?"

Jillian started ticking off points on her fingers. "Increasing profits, building morale, and bolstering self-esteem, to name a few."

"Do you think we'll be allowed to watch?" I asked.

Vance nodded. "This is a public area. If they didn't want any observers, then they shouldn't have ventured outside. Come on. Let's see how close we can get. I want to see who the dogs will single out."

Well, the answer to that question wasn't an easy one. They woofed at practically everybody.

Then again, the people were all moving around, so it was hard to pinpoint anyone suspicious. What the hell were they doing, anyway? Playing a game of tag? Have you ever seen a group of grownups laughing hysterically as they're chased around a grassy field? I was seriously tempted to record some of their antics and post it on YouTube.

"There's something you don't see every day," Jillian softly mused.

"They're acting like a bunch of idiots," Vance added. "What are they doing?"

I shrugged. I have never had any desire to work for a huge corporation, especially when they periodically held retreats and made their employees do that. But, I'm sure there was a legitimate, practical reason for it, or else they wouldn't be doing it. I will have to admit, it looked as though everyone was enjoying themselves. Perhaps that was the reason? To force everyone to get along?

Whatever.

I had been to this little park before. Granted, it was a few years ago, and I had been happily married at the time, but I do know how big an area this park encompassed. Plus, there were sidewalks running along the perimeter of the grass on three different sides, which consequently, were three different streets. Therefore, I felt I was able to approach the group from a different direction without raising any suspicions.

"Where are you going?" Jillian wanted to know, as she saw me straighten and wrap the dogs' leashes around my hand.

"I'm going for a little walk," I told her. I unwound Watson's leash and held it out to her. "I want to see if either of the dogs will react to anyone over there, so I need to get them as close to those people as I can. Would you care to join me?"

Vance was nodding. "Great idea. A couple is less likely to arouse suspicion. Go with him, Jillian."

"And what are you going to do?" my girlfriend asked, as she took Watson's leash.

Vance reached into his jacket pocket and pulled out one of those Bluetooth earpieces that had a distinctly cyborg flavor about it. He hooked it over his ear and waggled his phone.

"I'm going to pretend to be on the phone," our detective friend informed us. "Although, what I'll probably be doing is recording some notes about these people and watching you two like a hawk."

Satisfied, Jillian and I moved along. Delighted to be taken on a walk, especially when huge expanses of lawns were involved, the corgis immediately pulled us over to the grass. I couldn't blame them. Who'd want to walk on concrete when a much more comfortable option was available?

We headed east, back by the front of the hotel, and approached the fountain I had spotted from the hotel's front entrance. Sherlock moved as close as he could to the water's edge without sticking a toe in. The inquisitive little corgi sniffed a few times at the splashing water, then turned to look up at me, as though he was requesting permission to jump in.

"Not on your life, amigo. Push that thought out of your little puppy brain."

We walked around the fountain, all the while keeping the frolicking antics of the Semzar employees in our sights. Then, after a few more minutes of allowing the dogs to sniff the water, we angled north, and then slightly west, which put us on the same lawn with the group of people playing tag. At least, that's what it looked like they were doing.

As we walked closer, we started to get noticed. Not us, mind you, but the dogs. We started hearing all the telltale 'Ooohs' and 'Ahhs', and remarks stating how cute the dogs were. A few of the people even broke away to come meet the corgis, which was exactly what I wanted to happen. Sherlock and Watson sniffed and licked nearly a dozen different hands before we got our first hit: a tall, slim elderly gentleman, wearing a light grey stylish suit that had a shorter jacket and padded shoulders. The suit's pants were slim-fitting and snug, and I couldn't help but admire the guy for pulling off the look. Hell, I could never look that good in a suit. This guy was dressed to the hilt and exuded confidence. He had to be a Semzar executive of some sort.

"Those are some mighty fierce-looking watchdogs you have there," he quipped, as he smiled down at the dogs. He stretched out a hand, intent on ruffling the top of Sherlock's head.

Right about then, I noticed Sherlock's ears. They were flat against his skull and, if I didn't know any better, I'd say the little corgi had narrowed his eyes. It almost looked as though Sherlock was daring this guy to touch him. I was going to have to intervene, or else Mr. Fancy Pants here was gonna wind up with a dog bite and I would end up getting sued.

"Careful there, pal," I cautioned. "Sherlock hasn't been feeling too well today. He's been acting a little nippy lately."

The hand paused in its descent. After a few moments, the elderly man straightened and turned to look at me.

"Thank you for the warning. I appreciate your honesty."

"No problem," I said, as I nodded at the guy.

"Emil Gregory," the man announced, as he held out a hand.

Uh, oh. I couldn't give this guy my real name. What if he recognized the name Anderson and put two and two together? *Think, Zack. Think!*

"Hi, I'm Mike. Er, Mike Wadsworth."

Emil turned to Jillian and waited patiently for an introduction.

"Oh, I'm sorry," I sputtered. "Where are my manners? This is, er, Destiny Williams."

"A pleasure to meet you, Miss Williams. Your dogs are absolutely adorable. These are the same dogs the Queen of England prefers, are they not?"

Jillian nodded and gave each of the dogs a pat

on the head.

"They sure are. Welsh Corgi Pembrokes, favored by the good queen herself. Ain't that right, sugar?"

I quickly closed my mouth, which had dropped open the instant Jillian had begun to speak. Since when could she speak with a flawless southern accent? I grinned. That woman will never cease to amaze me.

"It sure is, babe. So, Emil, if you don't mind me asking, what are you guys doing? Besides running around like a bunch of lunatics, that is."

Emil turned to regard the mass of people who were busy sprinting from one side of the grassy field to the other, like a group of school children at recess. He gazed admiringly at them for a few moments before turning back to me. He gave me an evasive shrug and smiled.

"They're just blowing off some steam. It's not every day you see grown men and women act like that, is it?"

"No, it isn't," I chuckled. "I do believe I'm in the wrong type of work."

Emil slipped me a business card. "If you're ever looking for something new to do, do give me a call."

I looked down only long enough to see the words Semzar Pharmaceuticals written in gold ink across the face of the card.

"I will, sir. Thank you!"

"Ma'am," Emil added, as he turned to Jillian.

Then he wandered back to a small group of three men and one older woman to observe the antics of his employees.

"Come on," Jillian instructed, as she hooked her arm through mine and led me on a course which would skirt around Semzar's activities, but be close enough to get a better look.

"Since when could you talk with a southern accent?" I asked, as I dropped my voice to a whisper.

"Hey, I'm sorry! 'Destiny Williams' sounded like a southern girl. I was just playing my part. I assumed you didn't want to use our real names?"

I nodded. "Yeah, it just came to me, only I wasn't prepared for it."

"One would think writers would be able to think quickly on their feet," Jillian teased.

"Usually I can, but obviously I didn't back there. Wow. Talk about your mother-of-all brain farts."

Several more employees approached us and asked permission to pet either of the dogs. I noticed how none of the six or seven people who wandered over had tried to reach a hand down to pet either Sherlock or Watson. Had Emil given his people a warning? Either way, it didn't matter. Sherlock and Watson absolutely loved the attention, and didn't growl once at the any of them.

As I watched these strangers interact with my dogs, I tried to see if my mystery caller was contemplating an approach. I found her, only because she was one of the few red-headed women who were there, but she was nowhere near me or the dogs. In fact, it looked as though she was trying to keep as much distance as possible between us.

Oh, well. I guess I'll have to wait for her phone call to figure out who she is and what she wants. Or, better yet, what she has that she thinks I'd want. Maybe it was some dirt on ol' Emil over there? Perhaps some pictures of one of ye Almighty Upper Class in some type of compromising situation?

Man, I really do watch too many movies.

"How much longer do you want to stay out here?" Jillian asked.

I shrugged. "I really don't know. I'd like to get Sherlock and Watson over to that small group there, the one with our mystery informant. That's the only group that the dogs haven't had a chance to meet. You heard the dogs earlier. Sherlock was woofing like crazy, yet, so far, he's only singled out one person, and that was the guy in the fancy Italian suit."

"We're going to need some type of cover story if you want to wander over that way," Jillian was saying, as I hooked my arm through hers and led her toward the distant group.

Before I had a chance to respond, the Powers That Be dropped the perfect excuse in my lap. The game of tag had just finished and now three inflatable beach balls were produced. As soon as they were inflated, each group was tossed a ball, and it began to soar through the air as many of the employees smacked it as though they were playing volleyball.

As expected, both corgis watched the proceedings like hawks. I looked down at the leash I was holding and then over at Jillian. I swear Sherlock knew what I was about to do.

"Zachary, don't you dare!" she hissed at me.

I grinned at her and timed my move to correspond with the next time the ball went soaring into the air. As soon as Mystery Woman's group whapped the ball skyward, I loosened my grip on Sherlock's leash. The canny little corgi felt the slack and immediately took advantage of the situation. He gave a well-timed jerk on the leash and presto, he was loose!

Sherlock yipped excitedly and tore off after the ball. His sharp, piercing barks sounded noisily across the park as he ran full-tilt toward the closest airborne beach ball. Since the participants of the team-building exercise were now wearing bemused expressions on their faces as they watched Sherlock race toward them, and weren't paying attention to the point of the exercise, which was to keep the ball aloft, the ball started falling to the ground.

Sherlock appeared beneath the ball when it was less than three feet away from striking the ground. The tri-color corgi jumped up, which thrust his nose skyward. The ball rocketed back up into the air, on a direct intercept course with a blonde-haired woman. The lady giggled, clasped her hands together, and whapped the ball back over to Sherlock, only her volleyball skills were substandard. The ball curved west, away from Sherlock, who immediately doubled his efforts to be the one who intercepted the ball first.

A streak of orange and white whipped by me. It was Watson, only how she got away from Jillian remains to be seen. I turned to look back at Jillian for confirmation this was part of the plan, only my girlfriend had a look of helplessness on her face and was holding up both hands in a 'what can you do?' gesture.

"Okay, we have some new rules," a man's voice was heard shouting.

I glanced over at the small group of Semzar bigwigs and executives and saw that a guy roughly my age, standing next to Emil, was speaking.

"Try to avoid the dogs. If the balls touch the ground, or else the dogs manage to take control of them, then that group is out. Everyone ready? Go!"

There was a mad rush as people clamored forward, intent on getting the ball away from Sherlock, who always seemed to be under someone's feet. He seemed to know where the ball was going to land, and managed to situate himself before anyone knew what was happening. In fact, it only took about 30 seconds before a member of Mystery Woman's group (a young guy in his twenties) slipped on a wet portion of grass and landed on his butt. Hard.

Unable to keep the volley going, the ball

started falling toward the ground. Sherlock darted between one woman's legs, maneuvered around a large man wearing a black suit and tie, before reaching the fallen player. What he did next had me gasping with surprise.

Apparently, to better ensure the ball returned to the air, Sherlock decided to give the ball a hearty nudge in the right direction. How did he do that? By jumping onto the young guy's lap and launching himself into the air by bunching his legs and jumping off of his ... his ... hoo boy. That was gonna require some recovery time.

The man groaned and immediately cupped the family jewels. He rolled over onto his side and curled up into the fetal position. I also noticed wet doggy prints all over the guy's clothes. Once again, I had to hand it to the corgis. They may be low to the ground, and they may be the smallest breed of herding dog, but man alive, those stumpy legs had some power. From the way the guy was rolling around on the ground, you'd think someone had just stomped on his genitals. Then again, I guess Sherlock kinda did.

I will add, by the way, that it had to be the best jump I've ever seen Sherlock execute. He sailed gracefully through the air, with his two tiny front legs stretched out in front of him and his back legs sticking out from behind him, in full Superman pose. He landed nearly ten feet away, and was already en route to the next group. Watson joined him there and together, the two sprinted for the second group, who were staring at the two approaching dogs with slack-jawed looks on their faces.

Twenty seconds later, the dogs moved on to the third group. While I watched the corgis' hysterical antics, I couldn't help but wonder how the two of them knew they only had to touch the ball once. It's like they heard the explanation of the improvised rules for the game and were acting on it.

In less than two minutes, it was all over. None of the three groups had been able to keep their ball away from the corgis. Although, to be fair, the vast majority of them were still laughing so hard at Mr. Crushed Nuts that any form of communication was lost among them. Panting contentedly, Sherlock and Watson wandered back over to me. In fact, Sherlock circled around me and promptly sat by my right foot, like I had given the 'heel' command, which I hadn't. He knew it, sure, but usually wouldn't sit by my right foot unless I told him to.

Little showoff.

Shaking my head, I grabbed his leash and saw that Jillian had reclaimed Watson's. Then I heard the warning woofs from Sherlock and looked up. It would seem good ol' Emil was headed my way again. I also couldn't help but notice that Vance had made a complete revolution of the park and was now sitting at a nearby table, pretending to talk on his phone.

"Those are some dogs, Mr. Wadsworth."

"I'm sorry they interrupted your game," I began. "These two have to be the smartest dogs I have ever owned. As a result, they always seem to know how to get the better of me. Including, I'm sorry to say, knowing when I'm switching the leash from one hand to the other. That's how he got away from me."

"No apologies are necessary," Emil assured me, with a smile. He turned to his employees, who had started to gather behind us. "Guys and gals, I hope you're proud of your performance."

Forty heads began bobbing, and there were a chorus of "absolutely" and "you bet" coming from all directions.

"That was sarcasm, people. For Heaven's sake, you guys just got your asses handed to you by two little dogs! What simple method would have prevented your defeat?"

Crickets chirped noisily nearby.

"Communication, people! What happened to your communication? Is that not why we are all out here in the first place? Without it, we might as well be living in the Stone Age."

Emil thanked me profusely for participating in their event and then herded the group back toward their office building, which was across the street and about a block north. I tried to make eye contact with Mystery Woman, but she kept her head down and didn't once look my way. And yes, I know what you're thinking. I shouldn't have tried so hard to get her attention. I had no idea if she

86

was truly in danger or not, and now, for all I know, I probably exacerbated the situation. I could only hope that she would call me tonight, at our usual time.

Once the last of the Semzar employees had all gone, Jillian and I wandered over to Vance, who was still sitting at one of the picnic tables. He looked up and hastily pulled his cybernetic ear-piece out of his ear.

"Get some good shots?" I asked.

"Could you have been any more subtle?" Vance countered. "Jeez, Zack. We're trying to keep a low profile here, not draw attention to us."

"Yeah, yeah, I know. Sorry."

"Did the dogs react to anyone?"

Both Jillian and I nodded.

"That older fellow, in the gray suit. His name was Emil."

"Emil what?" Vance wanted to know. He was busy scribbling in his notebook.

"It's, uh, er, it's Emil ... something."

Vance stared incredulously up at me, "You forget the guy's name?"

"It's Gregory," Jillian helpfully supplied. Then she giggled at me and slowly pointed down at my left hand. "I do believe you're still holding his card, are you not?"

"Well, I'll be a monkey's uncle," I muttered, as I opened my hand to reveal the card. "I forgot about that."

I handed the card to Vance, who tucked it into a

side pocket in his notebook.

"At least it was only one person," I reminded everyone. "We definitely caught a break on that one."

"That was only about 40 people or so," Vance returned. "Semzar has over a thousand employees."

"How do you know that?" I asked, dumbfounded.

Vance held up his phone. "Because it says so on their website."

"Oh. Damn. That would mean..."

"We are going to need a quicker way to check everyone out," Vance answered, with a heavy sigh.

FIVE

For the record, I will say that I tried. I mean, I really, really tried to be awake at 3:30 a.m. However, I was no longer a spring chicken. How I ever managed to pull all-nighters back in college continues to floor me. In this case, I figure I made it to about midnight before the book I was reading—propped up in bed—fell to my chest. I know. When the phone woke me up, and I bolted upright, the book was catapulted across the room. It took me a little bit to find my phone (I purposely left it on the night stand) and answer it before the call went to voice mail. Using hands that felt like they were encased in lead (what, had I been laying on them?) I managed to take the call.

"H... hello?"

"Zack? Is this Zachary Anderson?" a female voice softly asked.

I cleared my throat. "Yup."

"Weren't you expecting my call?"

By this time, a few lights had finally clicked on upstairs and I realized who must be on the phone.

My brain lost its cobwebs and booted up. A glance at the bedside clock confirmed that it was, indeed, 3:30 a.m.

"Yeah. I mean, yes, I was expecting your call. Is this the lady from the hotel?"

"Yes. Don't you remember me, Zack?"

"Don't I remember you? Are you telling me that we've met before?"

"Yes! On several occasions. I was good friends with Samantha."

Something about that statement didn't add up.

"Wait a moment. If you and Sam were such good friends, then why did you wait so long to say anything on the phone? And better yet, how do you even have my cell phone number? I changed the number once I made it to Oregon."

"I have a friend who works for a major cellular carrier. It just so happened to be the one you and Samantha used. Logic suggested you'd keep using the same service, provided they offered coverage in Oregon. This carrier has the most coverage across the country, so I figured it couldn't hurt to look you up."

"So, why did you wait so long to say something?" I repeated, growing angry.

At that moment, the door to the suite's second room opened and Jillian appeared. An uncertain look appeared on her face, but was quickly dispelled once I tapped the chair beside the bed. She was wearing purple flannel pajamas and her hair, pulled back into a ponytail, was somewhat messed up, but I still thought she looked incredibly fetching.

"You have no idea what I've gone through, Zack. Actually, that should be, 'what I'm currently going through'. I'm afraid for my life. I'm watched all the time. In fact, I'm starting to think there might be people watching me day and night from across the street."

And I thought *I* watched too many movies. People don't really do that, do they? In this day and age? No way. However, my skepticism must have bled through the phone, because my mystery informant started getting defensive.

"Zachary, you have to believe me! With what I know about Semzar Pharmaceuticals, I could probably bring the whole company down. I'm telling you, I have to be careful. I don't trust anyone."

"If you're that worried," I sputtered, "then why don't you go to the police? Don't they offer protection in exchange for incriminating evidence? There's gotta be something they can do."

"Something tells me that if I should try going to the police, then I would be silenced. Permanently."

"What exactly do you want me to do?" I asked, growing concerned. "And tell me your name, would you?"

"If you don't remember it, then that might be a good thing. For me. Listen, I think I need to go. I'll be in touch."

"Wait! You're sure Semzar Pharmaceuticals had something to do with Samantha's death?"

"Without a doubt. She was killed because of what she discovered."

"Huh? She discovered something? What did she discover?"

"I'll tell you later. Listen, we'll have to meet again, but not until I can figure out how to do it undetected. I have something I know you'll want. Until then."

The call terminated, only I wasn't any closer to answers than before. If anything, I now had more questions, and they were questions I desperately wanted answered. What was this about Samantha discovering something? And whatever it was, was it really worth killing for? I couldn't even begin to imagine what it could be.

I took Jillian's hand in my own and we sat there, together, in silence. Jillian, to her credit, didn't pressure me to start talking. She simply waited.

"That was her," I finally said.

"I figured it was," Jillian said. "What did she say?"

"She wouldn't identify who she was," I slowly answered. "The only thing she really told me was that she was a good friend of Sam's, and that apparently, we had met before."

"Yet, you don't remember her, do you?" Jillian guessed.

I shook my head. "Nope. I haven't decided if I should be concerned about that or not."

"What did she tell you?" Jillian wanted to know.

I took a deep breath and leaned over to give Sherlock a friendly rub on his belly. Since this was the dead of night, Sherlock was out cold. Both he and Watson were on the bed, with Sherlock on his back, all paws up, and Watson snuggled up next to Sherlock. And no, before you ask, it wasn't that cold in the room. That's just the way they like to sleep when they're together.

"Well, let's see. When I asked her how she even had my cell phone number, she said she had a friend that worked for the cell phone company. I can let that one slide. Then she told me that she was afraid for her life. She was certain she was being watched, and even suggested there was someone across the street watching her at all times."

"Like a police stakeout?" Jillian asked.

"Exactly," I nodded. "But when I suggested going to the police, she seemed to think that would make things worse."

"I'm not sure how," Jillian admitted. "Go on."

"Then she told me that she was certain Samantha was killed because she discovered something. Something about Semzar. She wouldn't say what."

"Suggesting Semzar Pharmaceuticals has a shady past?"

"She didn't say, but that's the feeling I got from it. Oh, you'll love this next part. She wants another meeting."

"And she wouldn't say what she has for you?" Jillian asked. Her concerned expression morphed into a frown. "How cryptic. Do you think she could be leading you on?"

"It's possible," I admitted, "but I can't imagine what her motive would be."

"Well, what about if she was acting on Semzar's authority? What if she's only doing what she was told?"

I shrugged. "It's possible."

"Where do we go from here?" Jillian wanted to know.

"I'd say we start doing some research on Semzar. Ol' Red seems to think..."

"Ol' Red?" Jillian interrupted, as a look of confusion appeared on her face.

"Oh, sorry. Our mystery informant has red hair, so I kinda nicknamed her Red."

"I see. You were saying you'd like to do some research? On Semzar?"

I nodded. "Yeppers. I was thinking maybe we could hit up the library."

"I'll look forward to it," Jillian said, as she patted my hand encouragingly. She rose to her feet and gave me a gentle kiss goodnight. "I'll see you in the morning, Zachary."

The next day, at approximately 9:00 a.m., the two of us walked into one of Phoenix's many libraries. Their website claimed the Phoenix Public Library consisted of 16 different branches, which boasted a collection of nearly two million books,

DVDs, CDs, and various media resources. Surely, somewhere in that collection of data was something that would help us figure out why Semzar Pharmaceuticals would want my wife killed. If it was there, I vowed to find it.

"This place is huge," I remarked, as we walked in the main front doors. "Where do we even start?"

Jillian promptly walked over to a pyramidal kiosk that had illuminated diagrams of each floor of the library. And, for the record, this particular branch had three. Floors, that is. I told you it was big. Jillian studied the layout of the first floor and then tapped an area roughly northeast from our current location.

"Here. Do you see these two tables? That's where we'll find the public access computers. I'm guessing that's where we'll also find the terminals that have access to all the public records this library says it has."

I nodded. "That way it is."

We navigated our way around bookcases, walked by a huge reading area with row after row of comfortable arm chairs (many of which were occupied), and even walked by a section that had advertised audiobooks. This library had digital audio books. I stopped long enough to pick up a small device the size of a flash drive. This gizmo was equipped with a headphone jack, allowing the listener to plug the device directly into an audio system—or car—and listen to the chosen book, all without having to worry about changing CDs.

"Have you been in this branch before?" Jillian softly asked.

I shook my head. "I'm pretty sure this used to be a part of a mini-mall. I've been to Phoenix libraries, don't get me wrong, but I'm positive I've never been in this one before."

We passed by a row of bookcases, which advertised Recent Releases. Jillian suddenly stopped and pointed at a familiar cover on the top shelf.

"Look, Zachary! They have your latest book!"

I feel I should point out that most libraries are already, by nature, quiet. However, that one comment alone seemed to silence every conceivable sound, so that the only thing I could now hear was my own breathing. Noticing the complete absence of noise, I slowly turned around and surveyed the room. Every pair of eyes in the reading room, and I guessed there had to be at least two dozen, suddenly stopped what they were doing and were intently watching me. I noticed movement in my peripheral vision and saw that Jillian had placed a hand over her mouth, as though she had uttered a foul word.

"I think that was loud enough to be heard back in Oregon," I quietly observed.

"I'm so sorry," Jillian whispered back.

"It's okay," I assured her. "No harm done."

Just then, I felt a tap on my shoulder. Turning, I saw a tiny, wrinkled face peering anxiously up at me. Now, I say 'up' because she couldn't have been taller than five feet wearing heels. She was standing just behind me, and was peering intently at the titles, no doubt trying to figure out which one was mine. Several books were clutched tightly in her arms and, as she saw me look her way, she held up her selections.

"Is it one of these, dear?"

"You're looking for my books?"

"Yes, dear. I heard her say one of your books was here, in our library. I'm wondering if it's one of these."

I looked down at the two books she was holding. According to her selections, I was either Tom Clancy or I was Dan Brown. I leaned forward and tapped the cover to *Origin*. The woman's eyes widened with shock and wonder.

"No, I'm not Dan Brown," I hastily added. "I was just going to tell you that I've read this one, and it's not too bad. I liked *The DaVinci Code* better, though."

"Then, which one did you write, dear?" the woman plaintively asked me, as she shelved the two books she had been holding.

I sighed and tried to envision what her reaction was going to be. Looking helplessly at Jillian, who gave me an apologetic look, I leaned over and tapped the book with the bare chested man on it, with perfect abs, I might add. The elderly woman squinted her eyes as she pulled the book off the shelf. Once she read the title, and noticed the author's name, I saw those thin eyebrows of hers jump straight up.

"This? This is your book? How can that be? This one was written by a woman named Chastity Wadsworth."

"Please, lower your voice," I pleaded. "I write under a pseudonym. The books tend to sell better when the readers believe a romance novel was written by a woman."

A smile slowly spread across the woman's face. Her eyes twinkled with mirth.

"You really wrote this?" the woman asked again.

I nodded. "I did. And, I should warn you about something. That book you're holding isn't for the faint of heart. It has some, er, steamier than normal scenes in it."

"Done!" the woman exclaimed, as she clutched the book to her chest. "That's just what I needed to hear. Thank you, young man. Or, should I say, woman?"

The lady giggled as she moved off. Yeah, I'm sure I was blushing by this point. A quick look at Jillian had her holding her hand against my forehead with alarm.

"Wow, your face puts off a lot of heat. I'm sorry about that. I really should watch what I say around here."

"It's okay. I think I might have even made that woman's day."

"The terminal is just over here," Jillian said, as she pulled me around the corner and away from the shelves.

A simple computer screen, looking no different from the rows of public access computers, sat forlornly in a single cubicle. A glance around the area revealed there were two other cubicles, all with the single terminal. All of them, I might add, were empty.

I slid over a chair as Jillian took the seat in front of the machine.

"Okay, what should we search for first?" she asked.

"Well, what records does this have access to?" I wanted to know.

Jillian's fingers flew across the keyboard. The screen changed to display a double column of academic resources and magazines. Also on that list, I noticed, was the *Arizona Daily Republic*, namely the largest newspaper that serviced the Phoenix area. I leaned forward to tap the name.

"Try this one. It's the local newspaper. If we're looking for mention of Semzar Pharmaceuticals, then I'd start here."

Jillian continued to type. I saw that she entered Semzar Pharmaceuticals News in the search window and then hit Enter. Within moments, a huge long list of results appeared, including the most recent, dated from two days ago, which mentioned the drug maker was holding a retreat outside, in front of the hotel, in two days. Well, no big news there.

Jillian selected an entry from a month ago. Apparently, Semzar had reported their fiscal year earnings, and it was easily 300% higher than what anyone had thought possible. The profit margins were so high that there was talk about giving all the upper executives huge bonuses. I caught sight of what they were planning on giving the CEO, one Emil Gregory, and my eyes practically bulged out of their sockets. The CEO was slated to receive upwards of $100 million!

I whistled as I went down the list of names. Looks like the reporter couldn't believe the numbers either, and was questioning the logistics of handing so much money over to the company's elite, when he (the reporter) could think of many more practical uses for such large sums of money.

My eyes jumped back to the CEO's name. Emil Gregory. Since when does the company's top executive participate in silly team-building exercises? I mean, I had always envisioned corporate bigwigs as the golf-playing, rarely-in-the-office types. Could Emil Gregory be what he presented himself to be? A simple, caring boss?

Then I remembered Sherlock woofing at him. He never once singled out anyone else, but to be fair, we really didn't get a chance to do that. Instead, the little corgi had been a little preoccupied by keeping the inflatable ball away from the staff. Still, somehow—and I didn't know how—that Emil guy was involved with Sam's death. I just needed to figure out how.

"Wow," Jillian softly exclaimed. "Get a load of this. Did you know Semzar Pharmaceuticals is responsible for a number of drugs? Drugs that weren't particularly successful when it came to treating patients?"

I shrugged. "It's not unheard of, especially when that's what they're supposed to be doing. Making drugs."

The screen changed again. This time, a few pages from a prepared report appeared. Jillian zoomed in on the second page and then leaned back to make sure I could see it.

"Do you see this? It's a list of all the drugs Semzar has made in the last five years. Do any of those names look familiar to you?"

I leaned forward for a closer look. There must have been at least fifty names on the screen. And, for the record, none of them looked familiar to me. Granted, the only medication I ever took was maybe an aspirin or two, or at the most extreme, a few Advil, if I ever got a headache, but thankfully, I had my health. My medicine cabinet was remarkably bare.

"Not a one," I admitted. "Why? Do any of them sound familiar to you?"

Jillian shook her head, which flipped her brown ponytail from her right shoulder to her left. Right into my face, that is. My nose was instantly annoyed and I ended up sneezing.

"Oh, I'm sorry. Did I do that?"

I gave my nose a good rubbing and stole a glance at my girlfriend. She was sitting, with her back as straight as a board, at the computer and typing so fast she could have made an executive secretary green with envy. Once again, I counted my lucky stars that she agreed to come with me to my old hometown. I certainly wouldn't want to be doing this search by myself. I mean, I could, but where would the fun be in that?

"When is Vance meeting up with us?" I asked, as I pulled my seat closer to the computer screen.

Jillian paused in her typing as she speculatively eyed me, "You're sitting awfully close to the monitor. Are you having trouble seeing the print? Perhaps we need to get your eyes checked out?"

I both groaned and chuckled at the same time, "My eyes are good. They're just tired."

Jillian checked her watch. "It's only 9:30. Come on, Zachary. My grandmother has more energy in the morning than you do."

"Hardy har."

"Here's something interesting," Jillian suddenly reported. "I wanted to read about some drug Semzar was trying to market, but I clicked the wrong link. But, before I hit the back button, I saw this article about a lawsuit being dismissed."

That got my attention.

"What was it about?" I asked. "Was Semzar the one being sued, or were they the ones doing the suing?"

"They were the ones being sued," Jillian reported, as she skimmed through the article. "Some person, and it doesn't say who, filed a lawsuit against Semzar."

"What was the claim?" I asked.

Jillian read some more.

"There are a few passing references to medical assertions, but nothing was substantiated."

"It was dismissed," I guessed.

Jillian nodded. "Right. And here's another one."

"Does that one say what the lawsuit was about?"

"Let me see. More allegations, more depositions, but nothing specific. Why wouldn't they have more details on the case listed here?"

I looked over at the screen and tapped the company graphics on the report.

"I'll tell you why. It's because Semzar is the one who created this report. If there was something unfavorable to say, then you had better believe they aren't gonna say it here."

Jillian was nodding. "I see what you mean. Let me try a new search."

"What are you looking for?"

"Semzar Pharmaceuticals pending lawsuits."

I rubbed my hands together. "Oooo, good one." I watched Jillian type her query into the terminal. The screen updated to display the results. I leaned forward, eager to see what was found, only what I was looking at was an empty page.

"Not one pending lawsuit," Jillian confirmed. "That's disappointing."

"Take out the 'pending' word," I suggested.

Shrugging, Jillian removed the word from her query. The screen was immediately filled with a long list of hits. Surprised, we both skimmed through the results. Jillian tapped the bottom of the page, drawing my attention to a single line: Page 1 of 3.

"Seriously?" I said, as I looked at Jillian. "There are, what, 25 results per page, and there are three pages? That's incredible."

"It is incredible," Jillian admitted, "but not in a good way."

"We need to find out more about some of these lawsuits," I decided. "Something smells rotten here."

"Our source of information is Semzar itself," Jillian reminded me. "We are going to have to broaden our search if we want to uncover more details."

I looked over at the rows of public computers. I tapped Jillian's shoulders and pointed at an open station.

"Whataya say we move this here operation over there?" I drawled, using what I hoped was an adequate John Wayne impression.

Jillian giggled, collected her notes, and pushed away. Five minutes later, she had repeated her search, this time using Google. Boy howdy, once we got off of the Semzar servers, did the stories ever change. Turns out our friends at Semzar Pharmaceuticals had a really good legal team. We found scores of lawsuits, all detailing highly questionable pharmacological experiments, or the lack thereof, regarding a number of new drugs.

Well, new at the time.

During the ten years Semzar Pharmaceuticals had been in business, it was consistently in financial trouble. Not in the legal sense, at least not that we could tell. They had yet to develop a 'hit' drug. In fact, the company must have spent a fortune settling their lawsuits, seeing how their last three drugs had been dismal failures.

First up was some drug, which I can't spell (or remember), which claimed it could cure something called Restless Leg Syndrome. I actually had to look the problem up, 'cause I was certain that condition was imaginary. Well, I was wrong. Turns out RLS was a legitimate medical condition, in which the sufferer had the near irresistible urge to keep their legs moving, typically in the evening.

What did Semzar's drug do? Well, according to the lawsuits we found, the unpronounceable drug created blood clots in their legs. As you can imagine, that wasn't a good thing. Semzar's gaffe never made the news, but I'm almost certain that was because they paid a fortune to settle the individual cases as they appeared.

Next up is another unpronounceable drug, this one with lots of C's and D's in it. This drug was more notable, since its claim to fame was the ability to block and prevent the average cold. Since nearly everyone I knew dreaded catching colds, you can imagine how many millions of dollars Semzar must have made selling something with claims like that. However, the drug was pulled after it was revealed it actually prolonged the cold, not prevented it. Lawsuits were filed almost immediately, and Semzar was forced to pull the drug and issue refunds.

And finally, we learned about a pain-relieving drug which claimed to be up to ten times more effective than Advil, and what's more, it specifically targeted sciatic pain. At first, it appeared as though Semzar had found their Golden Fleece. This drug was actually working, and once word got out, sales of the drug skyrocketed.

However, it wasn't meant to be. One of the side effects of this particular drug, if allowed to build up in the human body, was to heighten nerve endings, thus ensuring that the slightest pin-prick would bring about excruciating pain. Semzar couldn't yank that drug out of the public's hands fast enough.

"How has this company managed to stay in business?" I wondered out loud. "They must have spent millions, if not billions, settling lawsuits to keep themselves out of trouble."

"Did Samantha ever tell you the name of the drug she was selling?" Jillian asked.

I was silent as I considered. Had she? Sam never really discussed her work with me, seeing how she knew I really didn't care for pharmaceuticals, nor about hearing what they were supposed to cure. Surely, though, she must have mentioned something to me in passing. There must be something buried away in my memories.

"There was something," I recalled, using a wistful voice. I closed my eyes and willed the thoughts to surface. "She was excited about the latest drug she was selling, stating something about helping a lot of people."

"She didn't tell you the name, did she?" Jillian guessed.

"On the contrary," I argued, "I'm almost certain she did, only I can't remember it. I'm sorry. Hey, can't we Google it and find out what Semzar's latest drug is?"

Jillian returned to the computer and pulled up the search engine. She asked the computer to confirm the identity of the most recent drug Semzar had been developing. And there, right on the page, was the answer: glucosoquin. My P.I. had been right.

As I read through Semzar's description of the drug's medical properties, I knew we had found our answer. Semzar had been proudly boasting to anyone willing to listen to them that this drug was the cure-all to a problem that affected millions of Americans. For that matter, millions around the world, too. As Alex Stokes had informed us earlier, glucosoquin, Semzar claimed, was the cure-all for diabetes. No longer would sufferers have to change their diet or do any exercise. One simple pill a day, for the rest of their natural life, would effectively cross off diabetes from the Top 5 Deadliest Diseases list.

Come to think of it, I do remember seeing some commercials on television, when Semzar had started making its boisterous claims. I think I remember rolling my eyes at it, only to have Samantha tease me about it later. This had to be the drug Samantha had been selling. I was sure of it.

Jillian suddenly tapped the screen.

"Zachary, do you see this? Sales of this diabetes drug have been so strong that Semzar Pharmaceuticals has made its first profit in over five years. The reporter goes on to say that this one drug alone has managed to pull Semzar back from the brink of bankruptcy."

I tapped the desk as I reflected on what we had just learned. The drug Sam had been selling was some new wonder drug? If it did what they said it could do, then no wonder the whole country was excited about it. Everyone always seemed to be looking for the easiest way to get something accomplished. Well, nothing was easier than taking a simple pill. Not being diabetic, I couldn't even begin to imagine how much hope this one drug must have given people.

Then my thoughts soured. Based on Semzar's track record, was there something diabolically wrong with glucosoquin? Could there be some yet-to-be-reported side effect that Semzar desperately wanted to keep quiet? If there was, then one could only wonder what Semzar would do to keep the news from going public.

"We definitely need to track down Vance," I

decided, as we both pushed away from the computer. "He needs to know about this."

Jillian pulled out her cell and tapped a few commands onto the screen. After a few moments, the cell phone chirped back, which caused her to smile. She pointed outside and urged me to hurry.

"I just texted Vance. He says he was just about to call a cab, on his way here, when I told him to stay put. We're going to meet for lunch."

"Has he found anything?" I asked, as we both piled into the white van we had rented.

"He didn't say, but it did sound like he wanted to compare notes."

Back at the Phoenician, we decided to order room service, at my suggestion. I had left Sherlock and Watson alone for several hours now, and I wanted to spend some time with them. Both dogs enthusiastically greeted us at the door to our casita. Sherlock, the little booger, managed to slip by me and made it outside. He stopped around a dozen feet from the door, spun around to look at me from a crouched position, and gave several high-pitched barks. Unfortunately for me, I knew the nature of that particular bark, having heard it on more than one occasion.

Sherlock wanted to play, and he was openly inviting me to join him. In this case, I think the little snot was daring me to try and catch him. Watson appeared in the doorway and cocked her head at her packmate, as if to ask whether or not Sherlock knew what he was doing.

Before I could take a step, or before Sherlock could bolt, we all heard a loud, repetitive chattering. Whatever was making the noise chattered four times, fell silent for five seconds, then repeated the noise. Already knowing what was responsible for the interruption, I immediately scanned the area, looking for the roadrunner that I knew had to be in the area.

There he was, and I do believe it was the same fellow from yesterday. He had a mix of brown and white streaked feathers and had a bright red spiky crest on top of his head. He stared directly at Sherlock, ruffled the feathers of his wings, and then made the chattering noise again.

Sherlock finally reacted. He woofed at the strange bird. However, the only thing that happened was that the curious roadrunner took a few steps toward my corgi. Surprised, I glanced back at Sherlock, who now had both of his ears sticking straight up, and was watching the bird like, well, like a hawk.

The roadrunner turned tail and fled, but since I have seen those birds move, I know he really wasn't fleeing. In fact, yep. The bird just stopped to see if he was being followed. Sherlock turned to look at me, as if to say, 'Well? What should I do?'

Jillian tossed me Sherlock's leash. She emerged from the casita, holding Watson's. I clipped on the leash just as Vance emerged from his own casita. My detective friend had a WTF look on his face as our little procession passed by, led by the roadrunner, of course. I shrugged as I passed him, and increased my pace.

Thankfully, our impromptu power-walking session only lasted until we arrived at the parking lot. Strangely enough, the roadrunner ran straight to our van, cooed invitingly, and then disappeared under another car. I was about ready to drop to all fours, so I could see under the vehicle, when I caught sight of Sherlock. Both he and Watson had stopped by the van and had lost all interest in their feathered friend.

Sherlock approached the van, sniffed the rear wheel on the driver's side, and then turned to look up at me. Moments later, his rump hit the ground and he was panting contentedly. Both of them were, for that matter.

"What's up?" Vance asked, as he hurried to catch up to us. "What's going on? Were you guys really following a roadrunner?"

"Yep," I confirmed, and pointed at the van. "The crazy thing led us to our van, waited until we arrived, and then scurried off."

Vance appeared to be at a loss for words. "I'm not sure what to make of that."

I then pointed at the dogs. "Look at them. They sniffed the wheel there and then promptly sat down."

Vance's curiosity had been piqued.

"Isn't that what they do when they discover something?" he wanted to know.

I nodded. I handed Sherlock's leash to Jillian

and then promptly squatted next to the wheel. I ran my hands over the surface, just to see if anything felt out of the ordinary. The only thing I discovered is that, if you are foolish enough to run your hands along the surface of a car's tire, then you deserve to have your hands turn black.

Scowling, and resisting the urge to wipe my hands on my pants, I decided to drop a little lower and look under the van's carriage. Perhaps the roadrunner had doubled back and was hiding under there? Getting down into a push-up position, I looked under the van. Nope, no birds.

However, before I straightened back up, a flash of red caught my eye. Grunting with surprise, I reached under the van, up into the wheel well, and pulled away a tiny one-inch black cube. It had a single thin antenna on it, along with the flashing red LED I had noticed. Turning, I held the device up to Vance.

"Dude, I think someone bugged our car!"

SIX

D estroy that thing," I ordered, growing angry. "Someone has been spying on us? Watching everywhere we go? Oh, hell no. That's not happening."

"I'm with Zachary," Jillian added. "I don't like knowing that someone, somewhere, is watching us. I say either we turn it over to the police or we destroy it."

About ready to drop the device onto the ground so he could step on it, Vance hesitated. He held the device up to his eyes for a few moments before he looked back at me. Then he pointed at the car.

"Show me exactly where you found it."

The two of us squatted next to the rear tire well on the driver side of the van. I tapped an area near the bottom, which was almost concealed by the brake assembly. Then, much to my astonishment, Vance reached in to replace the device. After making sure it was securely connected, he straightened.

"Vance, what the hell are you doing? I said we need to destroy that thing!"

Vance held up his hands in mock surrender. "Hear me out, Zack. Someone put that thing on our van. Clearly, they are worried about what we're doing. What do you think will happen if, all of a sudden, they discover they can no longer track our car?"

"They'll find another way to follow us," Jillian breathed.

I slowly nodded. "I get it. If they're gonna watch us, then it's best to be able to control where we go, and what we do, right?"

Vance grinned. "Exactly."

"But I don't want them to know what we're up to," I complained.

"And they won't," Vance assured me.

"How?" Jillian asked, puzzled. "If they're watching the van, and this is the only means of transportation we have, then we'll have to ... oh. Oh! I get it. Very clever!"

"What?" I demanded, as I turned to my girl-friend. "What's clever?"

"Think about it, Zachary," Jillian said, as she took my hands. "If they want to follow that car, then let them follow that car. I'm willing to bet Vance is planning on procuring another vehicle, am I right?"

Vance was already on the phone and eagerly nodded. While he arranged to have another car delivered to us here at the hotel, a thought occurred.

Suddenly, I was grinning like a dopey idiot. Jillian noticed my goofy expression and couldn't help smiling.

"What do you have planned?" Jillian asked. "You've got something up your sleeve, don't you?"

I nodded and pulled out my own cell.

"If someone wants to follow this van, then I say we lead them on a nice, long, wild goose chase. There should be ... Randy? It's Zack. Hey, I'm ... what's that? Oh, I'm doing well, thanks. Listen, you wanted to know if you could do anything to help us out. Well, I have a job for you, pal."

**

Once Samantha's brother had assured us he had all kinds of places to take the van, he pulled out of the parking lot and disappeared from sight. Jillian and I turned to Vance.

"You're up, amigo," I told the detective. "The van is off, going who-knows-where. We need another car. What do you have for us?"

Just then, we heard the roar of an engine. A white 2019 Dodge Challenger, with blue racing stripes, suddenly rocketed around the corner. The driver noticed the three of us and immediately veered over. A young guy, in his early twenties, hopped out of the car, leaned back into the interior to retrieve a metal clipboard, and then approached Vance.

"Are you the Oregon detective?" the kid asked. He consulted his clipboard. "Mr. Samuelson?"

Vance pulled his official police ID and flipped it open in response. A set of keys were tossed over, followed by the clipboard.

"Sign here, please. And here. This final page says you're accepting full insurance with a policy provided by the agency. All right, we're done. Please drop it off at the dealership once you've concluded your stay here."

"Where's the dealership?" Vance asked. "Sorry, kid. I'm not from around here."

"Do you know where Camelback is?" the kid hopefully asked.

Vance shook his head, but I held up a hand.

"I know where it's at. Which direction? East or West?"

"West," the kid answered. "We're right next to the I-17."

I nodded. "Not a problem. I know exactly where you guys are. Hey, do you need a ride back?"

The kid shook his head and pulled out his phone, "No thanks. I've got an Uber on the way."

Once the car deliveryman had left, we all turned incredulously to Vance.

"This?" I sputtered. "This is your idea of subtle? Come on, pal. That thing's a sports car!"

Vance chuckled and gleefully rubbed his hands together. "I know, right? I've always wanted to drive one of these babies."

"You just called the dealership and they agreed to deliver one of their cars to you?" Jillian asked, amazed. "How did you manage to pull that off?"

"I've got a friend who runs a car dealership," Vance started to explain. "He..."

"Here?" I interrupted, incredulous. "In Phoenix?"

Vance shook his head. "No, back in Medford. Anyway, he knows a guy who runs the sales floor in a dealership here in Phoenix. He's the one who arranged the use of the car."

"With full insurance," I added. "That'll cost a fortune."

"Don't worry," Jillian assured me. "I can cover the cost."

"Oh, like hell you will," I vowed. "I'll be the one covering the price, okay? It's no biggie."

"And that's how that is done," I heard Jillian say to Vance.

It would seem I just got played. Oh, well. I've always wanted to drive one of these things, too. I held out my hand to Vance.

"Keys, please."

"Oh, hell no," Vance exclaimed, hurrying over to the car and sliding behind the wheel. "This is my idea. I'm driving."

"Shotgun!" Jillian called, as she hurried over to the passenger side of the car.

That left the teeny tiny back seat for me and the dogs.

"This thing isn't the most practical," I observed, as I looked into the interior at the back seat. "I don't think I'll fit back there."

"I'll move my seat forward," Jillian told me.

"You'll fit."

Ten minutes later, we were cruising west on Camelback Rd, headed back toward Phoenix from Scottsdale. The high today was supposed to be around 95°F, and it wasn't quite there yet. Vance wanted to roll the windows down, but I shot down that suggestion even before he could finish the sentence. Besides, I pointed at the dogs, and told him it was way too hot to be cooped up like this for an extended period of time. There was a reason why the locals referred to the State of Arizona as the Land of Eternal AC.

"So, where to first?" Vance wanted to know.

"Stay on this road," I ordered. "There's a car dealership for practically every make and model on Camelback. I know there's an Audi dealership in there somewhere, I just don't know where. I think it's time we talk to an Audi tech and find out if it's even possible to remotely take over a car."

Vance nodded. "Sounds like a plan. Hey, where did you tell that Randy fellow to go?"

"Oh, he's heading to a few places throughout the city, then he said he'd take the van for a drive up to Prescott, which is about 90 minutes north of us."

Vance grinned. "Nice. How much room do you have back there?"

"Bite me, dude. My knees are in my face. The dogs are enjoying it, though." And why wouldn't they? They were in a car, going for a ride, while sitting next to me. This was their idea of a perfect day. "Just don't drool on the seats, guys. And Watson? Clench it up, girl. No dropping any bombs in here."

Watson was prone, from time to time, to getting a case of the farts. As per Harry's instructions, after all, he is PV's local veterinarian, I've been trying to get Watson to slow down when she's eating. However, old habits are hard to break, which means Watson usually scarfs her food down before I can even scoop Sherlock's food into his bowl. And, one of the drawbacks of eating that fast is sometimes air is swallowed along with the food.

Well, the air has gotta go somewhere.

Fifteen minutes later, we started seeing the dealerships. There, on the right, was a Cadillac dealership, complete with a selection of cars on the roof of their showroom. How the hell did they even get them up there? Next was the Toyota dealership on the left, followed by Volkswagen and Nissan. A Hyundai dealership appeared on the right, followed by a huge Chevrolet dealership. I whistled as we passed lot after lot of brand new cars.

Suddenly, both dogs perked up, as though they had scented something interesting. I gazed curiously at the corgis, wondering what was up. Outside, we were passing dealership after dealership, with no other discernible stores in the vicinity. Before I could say anything to Jillian or Vance, I felt the Challenger's throaty engine rev a few times and then start slowing.

"There's an Audi dealership on the right up ahead," Vance reported, as he took his foot off the gas. "It's not as big as the others, but it looks like it has a decent sized service center. Think that'll do?"

I looked down at Sherlock, who was now leveraging himself up and out of the seat so he could look through the windows. His little stump of a tail wagged with anticipation. Watson only had eyes for Sherlock, so I'm guessing whatever Sherlock wanted to do was fine with her. Had Sherlock been alerted to the dealership or was it something else?

"That must be the one," I decided. "Follow those Service signs."

The Challenger coasted to a stop just outside a gleaming brick building with five different service bays. Three of the bays were closed, but two were open. As soon as we all exited the car, and I had both leashes wrapped securely around my hand, we made for the customer service office.

"What can I help you with today?" an elderly gentleman, wearing a bright blue Polo shirt emblazoned with the name of the car dealership on the pocket, asked. He glanced outside and saw the Challenger. "If you're looking for the Dodge dealership, you passed it. It's about four blocks east. There's a bright purple Viper parked street side. It's hard to miss."

Vance looked over at me and inclined his head. I was the one who wanted to come here, so I was the one who would be asking the questions. Besides, Samantha was the one who had the Audi. Yes, I'd driven it a few times, but I didn't really care for it. I think it had too many bells and whistles for my tastes. Thinking fast, I sauntered over to the counter, handing the leashes to Jillian as I passed by her. It was about then that the technician noticed we had two dogs with us.

"Now those are some cute looking puppies. What kind are they? How old?"

"They're corgis," I said. "And, believe it or not, they're both adults. Hey, listen, I have a question for you. Could you tell me if my wife used this dealership for service? She had a 2017 Audi Q7. Granted, you probably haven't seen this car in a couple of years, but I'm hoping your records go back that far."

"The records here go back as far as the first day we opened," the technician confidently told us. He started tapping instructions on the screen. "What's your wife's name?"

"Samantha Anderson."

"And the make of the car again?"

"A 2017 Audi Q7. Blue."

A few seconds later, the technician, Carl by his nametag, was nodding.

"Yep, I see it right here. We last saw the vehicle November 16th, two years ago."

I paled and swallowed uneasily. November 16th? That meant Samantha had her car serviced a week before her fatal accident. Could someone here have done something to her car?

"Are you okay, sir?" Carl politely inquired. "You look like you've seen a ghost."

I had both Vance and Jillian next to me in a flash. Jillian took my hand in hers.

"Zachary? Are you okay?"

"November 16th, 2016," I repeated, as I turned to Jillian. "That was one week before it happened."

"Before what happened?" Carl asked, growing suspicious.

"Before his wife's car was involved in a fatal crash, pal," Vance curtly answered. "Can we have the name of the technician who worked on that car, please?"

"What is this, some type of murder investigation?" Carl asked, growing nervous. "We had nothing to do with any accidents."

"What's going on here?" a polite, but firm female voice suddenly asked.

We turned to see a middle-aged woman several inches shorter than Jillian, with pale blonde hair, approach us. Right off the bat, I noticed her name tag. She was Emily Varden, and she happened to be the Service Desk Supervisor. Emily patted Carl on the shoulder and indicated she would be taking over.

"What seems to be the problem?" Emily politely inquired. Her face was guarded, but not aggressive. Her posture indicated she was concerned, but more curious than anything.

Vance held out a hand, "Vance Samuelson,

Pomme Valley, Oregon. These are my friends, Zack Anderson and Jillian Cooper. They..."

A loud, eardrum shattering bark sounded, and I'm honestly surprised the windows still had glass in them. Vance sighed, rolled his eyes, and offered Emily a grin.

"Sorry. Down there are Sherlock and Watson."

Emily leaned over the counter and saw both dogs staring up at her. Her face softened immediately and she made cooing noises at the dogs.

"Aren't they the cutest things?" Emily gushed.

"They are," I confirmed, "and they know it."

"As I was saying," Vance continued, "we are here in town to investigate the unfortunate demise of one Mrs. Samantha Anderson."

I watched Emily's eyes flick over to the computer screen. They widened with surprise, as she no doubt noted the name of the file Carl had pulled up on the computer. Then she glanced over at me and her eyes widened even further.

"Yes, she's my late wife," I confirmed, before Emily could ask the inevitable question. "Look, ma'am. I'll be honest with you. My wife died nearly two years ago. Everyone thought it was an accident, including the police. Hell, that's what I believed, too, until..."

I deliberately trailed off, hoping that Emily would be hooked and be motivated to ask the inevitable question.

"Until what?" Emily finally asked, when I didn't continue.

"...until I watched a video shot by a guy with a camera on his dash. The footage showed my wife's Audi, careening off northbound I-17, down the median, and over to southbound I-17. It, uh, smashed headfirst into a semi-truck."

Emily's hand flew to her mouth in horror. "Oh, I'm so sorry, Mr. Anderson. Do you believe one of us had something to do with that?"

"Honestly? No. But, what I would like to do is chat with one of your technicians, preferably one who has worked on that car. However, if that isn't possible, then anyone familiar with that model will do."

"What are you hoping to learn?" Emily asked. I noticed a healthy dose of caution had returned to her voice.

"I'd like to know if it's possible for a car to be remotely hacked."

Emily's eyebrows shot straight up. "Hacked? As in, taken over? You think someone might have been able to force your wife's car into oncoming traffic?"

Vance and I both nodded.

"That's the theory," Vance confirmed.

"And all because of that video," I added.

"What about the video?" Emily wanted to know. "I mean, is this an ongoing investigation? Are you allowed to tell me?"

"The video which shows my wife's car plowing into a semi," I stated. "The guy who shot it was so shaken up that he's become paranoid behind the wheel. But, the reason I think it's proof that something was wrong with the car, was the simple fact that not once did Sam hit the brakes as she drove off the road. Not once did she slow down. Now, let me ask you something, Emily. If you suddenly swerved off the road and knew you were headed for oncoming traffic..."

"...on a freeway," Vance hastily added.

"...on a freeway," I amended, "wouldn't you be slamming on the brakes? Wouldn't you try to swerve out of the way?"

"So, you're suggesting someone remotely took control of your wife's Audi and sent it straight into the path of a semi-truck?" Emily slowly asked. "And on top of that, whoever was responsible also managed to disable the brakes?"

"That's what we want to know," I agreed.

Emily picked up the phone and punched a few buttons on the console, "Harrison, would you report to the service department front desk please? Harrison, report to service, front desk."

"We really do appreciate your help," Jillian softly told the customer service supervisor. "And for the record? I truly hope the answer to this is a resounding 'no'."

"You and me both," Emily admitted.

The door opened and admitted a middle-aged man wearing the same blue polo shirt the rest of the staff seemed to favor. He was wearing khaki pants that had stains on his pant legs, as though he had wiped the grease off his hands regularly instead of washing it off, and had tattoos covering both arms. He briefly smiled down at the dogs before navigating around us to approach the counter.

"These people are hoping to have a word with you," Emily formally told the mechanic.

Harrison slowly turned until he was facing us.

"Do I know you? Is there something I can do for you?"

"Harrison was the last technician from our dealership to look at your wife's car," Emily explained. "Perhaps he has the answers you're looking for?"

"Has something happened to your wife's car?" Harrison asked me, concerned. "Bring it on in. I'll be more than happy to get it up on the racks and see what we can..."

"This was nearly two years ago," I interrupted, as the mechanic took a breath. "I don't think you'll remember this particular car, but I thought it couldn't hurt to ask."

"I'll be honest with you," Harrison began. "I work on a lot of cars. I don't think I'll remember it, either. Can you tell me exactly when it was and what type of car?"

"November 16th, two years ago," I began. "And it was an Audi Q7."

"A blue one," Jillian helpfully added.

Emily rapped her knuckles on her monitor, getting the technician's attention, "I have her file here, in case it might jog your memory."

Harrison walked around the counter and was silent as he stared at the screen. He eventually looked up at me and gave me an apologetic shrug. "I'm sorry, I really don't remember this particular car. It says here I gave it an oil change and one of our 20-point inspections. Nothing out of the ordinary was mentioned. It's not surprising. After all, this car was less than 6 months old."

"Did this car have something called Driver Assist?" Vance asked.

Harrison nodded. "Correct. It's a feature designed to assist people who can't parallel park their car. Once properly lined up, Driver Assist will perform the necessary calculations to maneuver the vehicle into a perfect parallel parking job."

I nodded. "That goes along with what I was thinking. Now, here's the million-dollar question: can a car be hacked?"

I'm sorry to say that Harrison didn't even bat an eye. He nodded, without giving any consideration to the question. Emily, I might add, had clearly expected a different answer.

"What?" she sputtered. "You're telling me it's possible?"

Harrison sighed and leaned up against the wall behind the computer.

"This is why all the cars I own, or have driven, were made prior to 2005."

"What does that have to do with anything?" Vance wanted to know.

"Any vehicle manufactured in the year 2005 or newer has an onboard computer system that can be hacked," Harrison matter-of-factly stated.

The three of us collectively groaned, while Emily continued to wear a shocked expression on her face.

Harrison grinned and crossed his arms over his chest, "Let me guess. You'd like me to expand on that, wouldn't you?"

"I sure as hell would," I mumbled.

"Ditto," Vance echoed.

"I think I'd like to trade in my car for an older one," Jillian softly whispered.

"Computer scientists have been doing studies on this very topic for a while now," Harrison explained. Judging from the sighs and grimaces he was making, this was apparently a sore subject for him. "Once your car's computer has been hacked, then signals can be sent to the power steering, or the locks, or any number of systems to get your car to do something you ordinarily wouldn't want it to do."

"How?" I demanded. "How is that even possible?"

"Easy," Harrison answered. "Modern day cars will typically have somewhere between fifty to a hundred control units, which are essentially small computers. These units control many of the vehicle's functions, from power steering, to power windows, to the locking system, and even the brakes."

The four of us, including Emily, gave visible jerks as we all gasped with alarm. I sucked in a deep breath and held it. It was possible? Someone could have given Samantha's car the order to turn off the brakes? How horrible that must have been for her! To know what was coming, and not be able to do a damn thing about it, was almost unbearable for me.

I felt myself taking deep, ragged breaths and then noticed both of my hands were gripping the counter so hard that my knuckles had turned white. Vance was the first to notice. He clapped a hand on my shoulder, harder than he normally would have, to get my attention.

"Zack, are you okay? Do you need to wait outside?"

I ordered my hands to release the counter and then took a few steps back. The dogs were there in a heartbeat. Sherlock and Watson whined as they both craned their necks to look up at me. I squatted and draped an arm around each of them.

"I'm okay, guys. Thanks. I just got some alarming news, that's all."

I turned around to see Emily reaching for a bottle of water. She drained nearly half of it before she leveled a look at Harrison.

"Okay, if what you say is true, how do we make sure our cars are protected? I mean, can we go buy some anti-virus software or something?"

Harrison grinned, but sadly shook his head. "The manufacturers need to be held accountable for keeping their vehicles safe and protected. New technology is being created each day to try and keep consumers safe. Hey, did you guys hear what happened to Jeep in 2015? Researchers proved they could use the Internet to remotely take over their Cherokees. Commands were given to change the radio station, modify the climate, and then, with the complete cooperation of the driver, they issued commands to shut off the transmission, which caused the accelerator to fail while they were going over 60 mph. And this happened on a freeway."

"Holy shit," I softly breathed.

"Not good," Vance agreed.

"I'm definitely trading my car in for an older model," Jillian told me.

"Wait a moment," I said, as a thought occurred. "This Driver Assist feature only tells the car to parallel park, right?"

Harrison nodded. "That's right."

"So, then, it wouldn't be possible for the car to drive itself across the road into oncoming traffic, would it?"

Harrison shrugged. "If the car's onboard computer has been compromised, which means someone else is in control, and since the Audi's computer can control the steering system, then it can theoretically happen, yes."

"I'm liking this less and less," I groaned.

"Now that we know it's possible," Vance began, as he furiously jotted down notes in his notebook, "how easy is it? You say that *any car,* any make, any model, that has access to the Internet is vulnerable, so what would it take to hack one of these systems?"

Harrison held up his hands in mock surrender. "I'm a technician. The only computers I'm familiar with are the ones we use in the shop. I couldn't even begin to imagine what it would take. However, with that being said, I'd like to point out that I'm very happy driving my 1976 F250. Why risk it?"

We thanked Emily and the technician for his unsettling news. Not a word was said as we all climbed back into the Challenger. Jillian volunteered to ride in the back seat with the corgis, allowing me a chance to stretch my legs.

Once we were back on the road, I let out the breath I hadn't realized I had been holding. My face felt clammy and my hands were cold. For the record, I can't even begin to remember how long it's been since my hands were chilled. November 23rd suddenly popped into my head and I cringed. I stand corrected. Apparently, I could remember. It would have to be the day I got the news Samantha had...

Sorry. I veered again. For those that may not remember, I have a tendency of veering off topic. I'll try to control myself.

"Well, we know it's possible," Vance slowly began, as we navigated through the thick traffic on Camelback. "What I'd like to know is, how easy is it to do? I mean, can anyone Google instructions how to do it and become an instant hacker?"

I started shaking my head. "I doubt it. You heard what Harrison said. The cars don't just have one computer controlling everything, but essentially one minicomputer for every system. What did he say? Up to a hundred control units? No, I figure you'd have to be a computer expert to be able to do it."

"I wonder how many people *could* do it," Jillian wanted to know.

"Do what?" Vance asked. "Hack into a car? I'd like to think that number is small. You'd definitely need to know your way around a computer."

"A computer whiz," I agreed.

"You know this area better than us," Vance reminded me, as he glanced my way. He downshifted and zipped around an articulated bus, which had just pulled over to pick up some passengers. "Where can we find someone who might know how to hack into a car?"

I shrugged. "I don't know. We could always find the closest big corporation and ask their IT department. They usually have one or two know-it-alls on staff."

"A big corporation," Vance slowly repeated. "Which big corporation?"

"Any, I guess. Why?"

"What about a certain pharmaceutical company?" Vance carefully asked. "Would they have their own IT department?"

For the umpteenth time that day, my blood ran cold.

SEVEN

Later that evening found the three of us, er, the five of us, reclining in Vance's casita, listening to some soft music, and going over our notes for the day. The mood was somber and the room was quiet, until I looked up with annoyance. Someone had a loud whistle emanating from their nose and it was driving me nuts. I leaned down to look at the dogs.

Sherlock, as was always the case, looked up just as I looked down. He blinked his eyes at me a few times and then returned his attention to his chew toy. Watson was sound asleep, snuggled up against Sherlock's side. I held my breath and listened. The whistle didn't appear to be coming from either of them.

Now that I think about it, I didn't hear the whistle any more at all. Uh, oh. Was it me? I cautiously let out a breath. A blast of noise, reminiscent of a sharp note from a piccolo, sounded. Both dogs jerked their heads up and looked around the room. Aghast, I looked over at Jillian and saw that she was trying her best to suppress a giggle. Vance was staring at me, as though I was an alien from outer space. Then he stuck his finger in his ear and jiggled it.

"Dude, blow your nose or something. Damn. That made my ears ring."

"I'm allergic to something that's blooming out there," I decided, as I headed to the bathroom. "I don't remember having this many allergy problems when I lived here."

"Perhaps you've become too accustomed to Oregon's fresh air?" Jillian teased.

I returned to the living room and shrugged. "Perhaps. Man, I don't know about you guys, but I'm having a hard time trying to shake what Harrison told us."

"About all cars manufactured after 2005 being hackable?" Vance casually asked, as he looked up from his notebook. "Me, either, pal. Wait until Tori hears this. I've caught her eyeing a '79 Corvette Stingray that's for sale down the road from us. The last thing I want to do is give her any excuse to buy the damn thing. Do you know what kind of gas mileage those Vettes get? It's crappy, trust me."

"What are you worried about?" I asked my detective friend. "Corvettes don't have any backseats. It's not a family-friendly vehicle."

Vance was suddenly grinning like an idiot. He looked at me and gave me a high five.

"I didn't even think about that. Awesome!"

I lost the coin toss, so tonight's dinner selection was on me. The bright side to that was I got to choose where we were going to eat. In this case, being back in the big city suddenly paid off. Phoenix had some fantastic pizza joints, and I think it's time I had a good piece of pie.

Pie. Pizza. I have never figured out why some people refer to pizza as 'pie'. To me, pie was a type of dessert, like pumpkin pie, or key lime pie. At no point should the dessert pie be called a pizza. Then again, I just called the flippin' thing 'pie', so I really had no ground to stand on. But, I digress. Back to pizza.

After I made my selection, and ordered a pepperoni pizza for Vance, and a Hawaiian pizza for Jillian (I liked both), all from the convenience of my phone, I might add, I settled back against the couch and stroked Sherlock's fur. Jillian joined me on the couch and rested companionably against my right shoulder. She took my free hand in hers and squeezed it tight.

"I have no idea how you're managing to stay so calm," she confided. "Had I discovered Michael had been killed, and learned how it could have been premeditated, then I'm pretty sure I'd be freaking out."

For those of you who don't know, or don't remember, Michael was Jillian's husband, who lost his battle with cancer several years ago.

"How do you know I'm not freaking out?" I asked her, as I wrapped my right arm around her and held her tight. Sherlock paused with his chewing long enough to cast a neutral look at Jillian before resuming. "You saw me back there at the Audi dealership. As soon as that Harrison guy confirmed that someone could have theoretically shut off Sam's brakes, I almost lost it. But, as I was staring at the guy, imagining what it must have been like for Samantha, I realized something."

"What?" Jillian asked.

Vance paused with his note-taking to glance up at me.

"I want whomever is responsible for this caught. I want him prosecuted to the fullest extent of the law. No, scratch that. I think I want to see this guy suffer, like I suffered. If it turns out Semzar is responsible, and wanted to shut Samantha up permanently, then I want to know why and I want to know who is responsible. By that, I mean, I want to know who gave the order."

"We're gonna get him, buddy," Vance promised. "There's no way some corporate jerk is gonna get away with this."

With the temperature currently a very pleasant 84 degrees, and since the sun had set nearly an hour ago, the outside air had become absolutely gorgeous. Crickets chirped loudly. We heard the howl of a coyote in the distance, which surprised Jillian and Vance, but not me. They must've figured there was no way a coyote would be stupid enough to wander within city limits. However, all I had to do was point out that the Phoenician backed up against Camelback Mountain, and there were quite a few places for a coyote to roam.

And undoubtedly find dinner, I silently added.

Just then, Sherlock's head snapped up and he dropped the bone he had been chewing. Watson, for her part, cracked open an eye, saw that her pack mate was already investigating, and promptly went back to sleep. Sherlock then gave a few warning woofs.

"What's gotten him riled up?" Vance asked, as he rose to his feet. He looked through the open windows and then through the decorative steel security door on the casita. After giving the area a thorough check, he shrugged and sat back down on the couch. "There's nothing out there, fella," Vance told the corgi.

Sherlock, however, wasn't convinced. I watched as his hackles rose. I figured it was my turn to check, so I headed to the door to look out, only to come face to face with a woman wearing a pizza delivery jacket. We both let out a bellow of surprise, which set Sherlock off with his barking.

"Sherlock, you need to be quiet, pal," I told him. "And relax. It's the pizza man. Er, woman. Sorry."

The woman didn't say a word. She opened up the large, insulated bag keeping the pizzas warm and pulled out several pizza boxes. She handed them to me and immediately turned on her heel and left, all without saying so much as a single word of greeting. Nor did she collect—or ask for—

any money.

"It's a good thing she didn't stick around for a tip," I mumbled, as I retreated back into the casita. I hefted the boxes and nodded appreciatively. Nothing makes a hungry man happier than having a thick crust pizza loaded with toppings, just waiting to be consumed.

Jillian suddenly held up a couple of twenties.

"I was going to take care of dinner tonight, Zachary. How much was it so I can reimburse you? I wasn't paying attention."

I shook my head. "She left so quick that I kinda forgot about paying. I've ordered so many pizzas online where I pay for them right then and there that I didn't think about it. That's weird, right? Who would deliver pizzas without getting paid for them? That doesn't make any sense."

Vance shrugged, pulled out a paper plate from the stack we found in the casita's tiny kitchen, and helped himself to several slices of pepperoni. I was in the process of handing Jillian a plate with several pieces of her Hawaiian pizza on it when I caught sight of another pizza box, sitting underneath the pepperoni. Confused, I turned to look at Vance, but he wasn't paying me any attention, as he was too busy wolfing down his pizza and going over his notes.

I know I didn't order any breadsticks, or wings, or anything like that. Perhaps the pizza place goofed? I was ready to ask Jillian when I saw that she had been waggling a finger at the dogs. After

Sherlock whined with exasperation, my girlfriend looked down at the two corgis and sadly shook her head.

"I'm sorry, guys. The answer is no. Ham is too salty, and is not good for you. I can't give you any of this. I ... Zachary? Is everything okay? What's the matter, don't you like the pizza? I thought you told me your favorite was Hawaiian, too."

"It is," I said, as I set my plate of uneaten pizza down on the coffee table. I pointed at the third box. "What's in that one? I only ordered two, namely the pepperoni and our Hawaiian."

"They probably made an extra one by mistake and figured they'd make our night by giving it to us," Vance said, without looking up. "It's happened to us a few times. The girls think an extra pizza, free of charge, is the greatest thing since the invention of peanut butter."

Vance and Tori's two girls, Victoria and Tiffany, would say that about any type of free food, I thought with a grin. Then again, who wouldn't? Curious, and partially hopeful there might be a third pizza in the box and not an assortment of plates and napkins, I cracked the lid and peeked inside. Never in a million years would I have guessed the contents. I thought the pizzas felt heavy. Now I knew why.

A sleek, state-of-the-art laptop sat nestled within the box. Written with a black permanent marker on the underside of the lid was a string of characters I knew all too well: aoatmaobt.

Now, to the outside observer, that would look like nothing but gibberish. However, I knew it for what it was, a password. This was Samantha's work laptop! How in the world did the delivery driver get it?

Wait. The driver! It had been a woman, and now that I think about it, the woman's hair had been red, and almost concealed by the baseball cap she had been wearing. That meant our driver had been Red, the mystery informant! Dang, I had wanted to talk to her!

So, what was she doing, posing as a pizza delivery driver?

Sorry, that was a rhetorical question. Her earlier message had said something about trying to find a way to get me something. Clearly, she had been talking about this laptop. She obviously believed she was being watched, and was taking no chances about being caught. How she knew we had ordered pizza was beyond me. Could she have been watching us? Could she have intercepted the real pizza delivery guy and arranged to deliver them herself?

I sighed. The world may never know.

Anyway, what about that gobbledygook password, you ask? It was an acronym for one of Samantha's favorite sayings: *As old as the mists, and older by two.* Red had given me Samantha's password, in case I didn't know how to unlock Sam's laptop. In my defense, I probably could have guessed it, but not before the computer would have locked itself up tighter than a drum, figuring someone was trying to launch a brute force attack on it.

I gingerly took the laptop out of the box and held it out, as though it was the Holy Grail itself. How many times had I seen Samantha typing away on this thing? Or working on this laptop until the wee hours of the morning? This device, I knew, contained lists of all her contacts and more than likely, records of her many sales. No, I had never seen it for myself, nor had Samantha ever confided in me what was on this thing, but what you have to understand is, I know my wife. Er, late wife. She was the epitome of OCD. She kept meticulous notes about everything.

She would have kept notes about when she called, how long she was on the phone, who the client was, and on and on. No wonder Red had kept this hidden. No wonder she thought she was being watched. She was evidently right! If this laptop contained what I think it did, then Semzar Pharmaceuticals would stop at nothing to get it back.

"What's that?" Jillian finally asked, as she looked up from stroking Sherlock's fur. "Is that a laptop? Where'd you get it?"

"It was in the third pizza box," I declared.

Vance's head snapped up so fast that I swear I heard his neck crack.

"Would you run that by me again?"

I pointed at the empty third pizza box, "It was in there. Remember, we ordered two pizzas, right?"

"Whose is it?" Vance wanted to know.

"Samantha's," I softly answered. "It's her work laptop."

"What?!" Vance sputtered, as he scrambled to his feet. "How in the world did that pizza driver know to deliver that to you?"

"I'm pretty sure the driver was Red, the mystery woman who has been calling me at 3:30 a.m. every morning. She said she had something she knew I'd want, remember? This has got to be it."

"What's that word there?" Jillian asked, as she caught sight of the open box and the underside of the lid. "I can't quite make out what it says."

"It's an acronym," I answered. "It serves as Sam's password. 'As old as the mists, and older by two'. We used to say that to each other all the time."

Vance hastily set his notebook to the side and made room on the coffee table.

"Let's fire that baby up. I want to see what's on it."

I helped myself to a few slices of pizza while the laptop booted up.

"Do you know what we're gonna find?" Vance asked.

I shrugged. "Not really, but I'm sure I can guess. Sam was always on this thing, sometimes for hours and hours on end. If she was selling that gluck ... gluco ... that wonder drug, then I'm sure she kept some very detailed notes on how much she sold and who purchased it."

"This thing is gonna be worth its weight in gold," Vance cackled.

A familiar prompt appeared. The computer was demanding the password before it would boot any further. I carefully typed the letters in and watched as the laptop beeped merrily and continued to boot into the desktop.

The wallpaper appeared, which was a picture of me and Sam trying our luck with a selfie, only Samantha had her hands over her mouth and was clearly in the midst of giggling. Poor Sam could never figure out where she was supposed to look, which boggled my mind since all you had to do was look at the lens. That was the picture looking at me now. An overwhelming feeling of sadness washed over me as I gazed at the picture of my dead wife. Never in a million years would I believe I'd be where I am today. Living in another state, owner of a winery, owner of two pint-sized dogs, and starting another relationship with a woman every bit as attractive as Sam had been, and just as intelligent.

"That's a wonderful picture of you two," Jillian softly told me. "Can I ask what she was laughing about?"

"Her inability to take a selfie," I answered, as a smile appeared on my face. "We tried several times, and she always ended up looking in the wrong direction. After the third time, she couldn't stop laughing, which was when I took the picture."

"May I?" Vance inquired, as he held out his hands.

After a few moments I nodded, and slid the laptop over to him. The detective glanced at the screen and jotted a few notes down. Then he started clicking on folders, of which there were many.

"Here's one that's simply entitled, 'Clients'. Let's see what's in that one. Hmm, looks like we have several sub folders. One says 'graphics', but the only thing I see is generic medical clip art."

"Weird," I decided. "I wonder what she needed that for."

Vance shrugged. "You'd know better than I would. Okay, this one says 'Misc.' I see some text files, which look like they were copied and pasted from various medical sites. Here's something from WebMD."

Jillian stood behind Vance and stared at the screen. She leaned forward to tap one of the icons.

"This one is a database file."

Vance leaned forward and squinted at the insignificant icon.

"How can you be sure?"

"I have a variation of this program in my store," Jillian answered. "I use it to keep track of new cookbook titles that are released from Amazon."

Vance immediately double-clicked the icon. There was a two-second pause before the computer beeped and brought up another password prompt. Vance grunted irritably, glanced over at the pizza lid, and carefully typed the same password as I used to boot into the desktop.

Almost immediately, the laptop buzzed angrily and the prompt reappeared. Clearly, the acronym was not the database password. Vance slid the laptop over to me and gestured at the screen.

"Think you can crack her password?" my detective friend asked me.

I stared at the screen and thought about what passwords I knew Sam had used. After the second incorrect attempt, the program promptly informed me that, if a third incorrect answer was entered, then the database would become locked and would require the user to contact the software-maker's technical support line to unlock. Swell.

I looked down at the keys and tried to imagine Samantha sitting here, typing away on her laptop. What password would she have chosen? Would it have been something that could have been guessed by an outsider? Or would it have been something known only to her? If I knew Samantha, and I did, then she would have chosen something significant to her, and more than likely, us.

Suddenly, I realized I knew the answer. I leaned forward and carefully typed in, *alwaysandforever*. Now, if you think that's a strange password, then clearly you've never been in love. Samantha and I almost always said 'always and forever' after saying I love you to each other.

Yeah, yeah, I know. It's sappy. But, do you know what? I don't care.

The computer softly chimed and the screen changed to show a list of choices.

Enter new record
View existing records
View reporting

I slid the laptop back over to Vance, who was now rubbing his hands excitedly.

"Way to go, Zack! All right, let's see what we have here. Existing records? Let's take a look. Damn, you called it, pal. It's a database, and she has notes on just about everything."

"She even noted the difficulty of the sale," Jillian observed, as she read the screen over his shoulder. She slowly nodded. "I'm really liking how Samantha's mind worked, Zachary. She took some very detailed notes. Look at this record. It's a doctor's office in Tempe. It says she spoke with both the doctor and the office manager, and it was the office manager who offered the most resistance."

"That will definitely come in handy," Vance said, as he scribbled more notes. He closed that record and opened another. Leaving the database open, he minimized the screen and clicked on another folder, this one titled 'Concerns'. His eyes widened with surprise as he started opening web pages Samantha had saved onto her computer.

Trying to find certain web pages, after you've originally found them on the Internet, can be like trying to find a needle in a haystack. Therefore, the makers of practically all web browsers have several ways to locate those specific web sites again. First, and the most popular, is to simply bookmark them. The browser notes the web site's URL and will take you straight back there once the link is clicked. However, that's assuming the web page still exists. If, for some reason, the web page is taken down, then you'll get the standard 'this page cannot be found' message.'

The second option is lesser known. Most browsers have the ability to save a complete copy of the web site to your local computer. Everything you see on the screen will then be bundled up and stored in a single file, or several files depending on how it's saved. That way, if the web page were to disappear, then the data wouldn't be lost, because a copy of the data would be sitting on the viewer's computer.

That's exactly what Samantha had done with a variety of websites. Sure, that takes up room on a computer's hard drive, but apparently she thought it was worth saving. Reading over Vance's shoulder, I could see no fewer than two dozen web pages had been saved onto Samantha's laptop.

Vance clicked the first one.

The browser opened and the web page appeared. It was an informational page, outlining the history of the flu, its warning signs, and what the symptoms were. Chills, coughs, sore throat, body aches, fatigue, and headaches were just a few of the wonders waiting for you if you were unfortunate enough to contract the flu. No wonder so many people lined up to get their flu shots each year.

One saved web page was from a local clinic, but as I noticed the town, my eyes shot open with surprise. Plano, Texas? That was an odd page to save.

I watched Vance open several others. The next three were also from small doctor's offices, only each of them were from a different city. And a different state, for that matter. One was from Twin Falls, Idaho, while another was from Bar Harbor, Maine, and the third was from Rocklin, California, which is a suburb of Sacramento. What those locations had in common was beyond me, at the moment.

"It looks as though Samantha was researching something," Jillian observed. "I just don't know what."

"That makes two of us," I added. "Vance, go back to the database, back to that list of records. Yeah, right there. Do you see how each one shows the name of the company, or doctor, and then shows where they're located? See if you can find one from one of those four places."

Vance nodded. "Roger that. This might take a while. There are over 7,500 records in here. Your wife was clearly a helluva salesperson, Zack."

"She was good at her job," I agreed.

Movement in my peripheral vision had me looking to my left. Sherlock had abandoned his chew toy (again) and had wandered over to the nightstand to the left of the bed. The corgi looked at the open, lower compartment of the night-stand and thrust his nose forward, as though he was looking for something. A few moments later, I heard a soft thud as something fell to the ground.

"What are you doing?" I asked, as I rose to my feet. "Keep your nose out of there. That stuff doesn't belong to you."

"What is it?" Jillian asked.

"Sherlock pushed the phone book off the stand there and onto the floor. I'm not sure what he's doing. Knock it off, you knucklehead. Umm, scratch that. Poor choice of words. Leave it alone, 'k? It's not yours."

I replaced the phone book, took two steps back toward the couch, when I heard the telltale thud. Turning, I saw that Sherlock had knocked the phone book off its perch again. And, to top it all off, the corgi was regarding me as though I was once more wearing my Dunce cap.

I slowly looked down at the phone book. It had fallen upside down, so now I was looking at the back cover. On the back cover was a glossy advertisement for a law firm which specialized in personal injury cases and wrongful death law-suits. Holding the book in my hand, I turned to my friends and waggled it in front of them.

"What?" Vance asked, as he looked up. "It's a

phone book. What about it?"

"Sherlock knocked this over. Twice. It landed so that I could see this. Significant?"

Vance took the book and studied the advertisement. His eyes traveled over to Sherlock, who was intently watching him. Then his gaze dropped down to the computer and the database he had been querying.

Without saying a word, Vance dropped the phone book on the table next to the laptop and began typing some commands. A series of results popped up in a second window. Vance closed that window and tried another set of commands. The second window then reappeared, with the exact same list of records which matched his search.

"What is all that?" I asked. "Since when do you know so much about databases?"

"Since I use them on a daily basis," Vance reported. "The program might be a little different, but they all have the same functionality and work the same way. Now, look at this here." He tapped the screen. "The first screen was a list of results which searched for the word 'glucosoquin'. Then I did another search, only this time I added the word 'death'."

"The same amount of records came up," Jillian said, appalled. "Is this glucosoquin responsible for killing people?"

Vance shook his head. "Not according to the vic's records. However, I can't help but wonder about the correlation. It looks like all the glucosoquin sales also have the word 'death' somewhere in the notes."

"Pick one," I instructed. I then pointed at the screen. "What about that one? It's from some clinic in Anchorage, Alaska. Read the notes. What does it say about that gluco-crap?"

Vance skimmed through the file. "Samantha sold the clinic twenty doses of the drug. The doctor on staff, one Dr. Thomas, took his patient to Canada, so he could administer the drug to the patient. And, it looks like this guy was in his fifties."

"The patient or the doctor?" I asked.

"The patient," Vance answered.

"Does it also have the word death in the file somewhere?" Jillian wanted to know.

Vance was silent as he read. After a few moments, he tapped the screen.

"Bingo. Here it is. Looks like the patient was seen at a clinic back in the States and was then admitted to the local hospital's ER."

"Why?" I wanted to know.

"The notes says the patient passed away from complications due to the flu."

Memories of the saved web page detailing the symptoms of the flu flitted through my mind. Coincidence?

"Was this directly after administering the drug?" Jillian asked.

Vance shrugged. "I don't know. It doesn't say."

Jillian leaned forward, "Yes, it does. Look above the Notes field and to the right. Samantha noted the date the patient was started on the drug. Do you see the death date? It was about three months."

"Then it can't be related to the drug," I decided. "I would think if the patient had some type of reaction to it, then it would have done so right from the start."

"True," Jillian admitted. "However, you never know with these new-fangled drugs anymore. The side effects are laughably ridiculous. Perhaps someone should have run a longer test on the drug?"

Vance moved to another of Samantha's sales. This time, he found a 24-hour clinic from Twin Falls, Idaho.

"Twin Falls," Zack commented. "I've been there before. It's right next to the Snake River Canyon in the southwestern part of the state."

"What do the notes say about this one?" Jillian asked.

"The vic sold ten doses of the drug," Vance began, "and it was..."

"Twenty to the first one, and only ten for this one," I recalled. "Does it say how much the drug was sold for? This had better not be one of these super-expensive drugs that only rich people can afford."

Vance fell silent as he searched for an answer.

"The Idaho clinic was charged $350 per dose."

I cringed. "Ouch. Yeah, I've heard worse, but wow, I've heard of a lot better, too."

153

"Just a moment," Vance added, as he held up a finger. "The clinic in Alaska was charged almost $750 per dose. That's more than double. What the hell for?"

"Where in Alaska?" I asked.

"Anchorage," Vance answered.

I pulled out my phone and did a quick search. A nagging thought had occurred, and I was pretty sure I had the answer. After a few moments, my suspicions were confirmed.

"It's based on population," I announced, as I held up my phone. "Anchorage's population is nearly 300,000 people. Twin Falls is considerably smaller."

"How much smaller?" Vance wanted to know.

"Well, hey, it's Idaho after all," I reminded him. I punched in another search. "Nearly 50,000 people."

"The prices are based on population?" Jillian asked, confused. "I don't understand why that would be."

"Maybe Semzar was expecting the larger cities to be able to afford it more than those with a smaller population?" Vance suggested. "I'm not sure."

"So, what happened to the Twin Falls clinic?" I asked.

Vance read through the file, "Let's see. This patient was given glucosoquin and was eventually admitted to the hospital, too."

"After how long?" Jillian wanted to know.

"Eight months," Vance reported.

"Well, it's not the drug, then," I deduced. "I would think the time frames would be close enough to be similar."

"What about symptoms?" Jillian asked.

"The clinic said the patient reported full body aches and a cough that refused to go away."

"Oh. You're right, Zachary. They couldn't be caused by Samantha's drug."

Vance started shaking his head. "*Au contraire, mon frere*. There is a similarity."

I shrugged. "And that would be...?"

"More flu symptoms. Body aches and coughs can be caused by the flu. Trust me, I should know. Victoria caught the flu several months ago and she went through hell trying to shake it. Body aches and coughs were just a few of the symptoms. Then she gave it to everyone in the house. Talk about the week from hell."

"How old was this patient?" I asked.

"Late thirties," Vance reported.

"Thirties for this one and the fifties for the other," I recalled. "That really doesn't help us, does it?"

"It's just too coincidental," Vance continued. "I mean, look at this. It looks like every clinic the vic made a sale at, and we're talking this glucosoquin junk, has some mention of something happening. I think it's evident that Sam thought something was up. Why else would she start taking notes like this?"

"You didn't know my wife," I told Vance. "That's the kind of person she was. She was very observant. She took notes about everything."

Vance punched a few keys on the keyboard. The screen changed again, and this time pulled up a different list of results. The detective let out an exclamation of triumph and motioned for the two of us to get closer.

"Here. Do you see this? What does this say to you?"

I looked at the screen. Another list of results were displayed. According to the report Vance had generated, the sales were of a mixture of other drugs, all from nearly two years prior to her switching over to glucosoquin. I shrugged at Vance. However, Jillian was also nodding. Whatever Vance had noticed, Jillian had noticed it, too.

Jeez. I was starting to think I needed to go back to school. I couldn't be this dense, could I?

"Look at the notes field, Zachary," Jillian instructed. "Look how short they are."

Comprehension finally directed a few rays of understanding my way. Those other drugs Samantha had been selling clearly hadn't aroused any suspicion. Well, nothing noteworthy, anyway. But glucosoquin? She had a minimum of two paragraphs of notes for each entry. Vance was right. Samantha had suspected something was wrong with the drug, and from the looks of things, she had started her own investigation. Why, then, had she never asked for my help? Why hadn't she told me anything about it?

The mystery woman, Red, came to mind. If, by chance, there was something seriously wrong with glucosoquin, and Samantha had started causing trouble, then Semzar could have taken action against her. Then again, could that have been precisely what had happened?

"What was Samantha's last entry?" Jillian asked.

I nodded. It was a good question. I just hoped the answer wouldn't cause me nightmares. And, for the record, it did.

"All right," Vance said, as he typed commands into the computer. "Give me a sec. I just have to sort by date modified and ... here we go. It's an entry in the notes field, dated from the 22nd of November."

"One day before her accident," Jillian whispered, in shock.

"What's it say?" I hesitantly asked.

"Just that she was taking her findings and was going to sit down with her boss and show him what she had found."

"With Semzar," I guessed, scowling as I did so.

Vance nodded and spun the laptop around so that I could see the screen, "Yep. That's exactly what she was planning on doing, and now there are no more entries. Coincidence?"

Jillian squeezed my hand tightly in her own as she felt me take several deep, calming breaths. Vance looked up at me and then grinned.

"Do you know what this means? Someone at Semzar Pharmaceuticals knows there's something wrong with glucosoquin and is desperately trying to keep it quiet. That means we've got to flush this guy out of hiding."

EIGHT

S ometime later that night, after everyone
had retired for the evening, something
pulled me out of a deep sleep. The bed was softly
shaking, and it took me a few minutes to figure out
why. Both corgis were awake, and both appeared
to be pacing around the confines of the bed.

"What are you two doing?" I quietly asked the
dogs. "Stop that. Go back to bed, okay? There's absolutely no reason for you two to be awake."

Have you ever tried to give a dog an order in the
middle of the night? Did it work for you? No? Well,
here's an unsurprising news flash: it didn't work
for me, either.

Then Sherlock started whining, as though he
was eager for something to happen. Maybe he had
to go outside to go potty? I was finally able to clear
my eyes and focus on the clock on the nightstand:
5:25 a.m. I turned to look down at Sherlock, who
continued to pace restlessly on the bed. Watson,
for her part, was sitting directly on her rump in
the middle of the bed, watching Sherlock wear a

path in the rumpled comforter.

I groaned again and reached for my clothes. That's just peachy. Obviously, the dogs needed to go potty. That meant I had to make myself presentable, which meant I had to stumble about like a blind man while trying to quietly find my clothes. Once properly attired, I clipped the leashes on the dogs and reached for the door handle. Right about then, both dogs lifted their heads and kept their ears pointing straight up. Sherlock's hackles were raised and I could tell he was moments away from barking.

"Knock it off, Sherlock. You will not be barking in here, thank you very much. Jillian is sleeping in the other room. Do not wake her up, okay?"

Once again, my concerns fell upon deaf doggy ears. Sherlock started barking like crazy, as though he believed the Boogeyman himself had just walked into the room. Naturally, that worked up Watson, who also started barking. I tried valiantly to shush them both up, but to no avail.

Jillian's bedroom door opened. Her hair was tousled, she was wearing one of the fuzzy gray robes the hotel had provided, and she was staring at me with a confused expression on her face. Before she could say anything, I angrily pointed down at the dogs.

"I don't know what has set them off," I grumbled, as I pulled on my shoes. "I'm going to take them outside and see if they have to go potty. If not, then I'm about ready to tell them to…"

I trailed off as I had just managed to open the door and was forcibly yanked outside, as though the leashes I had wrapped around my hand had just been attached to a team of horses. I was physically pulled out of the casita and I'm ashamed to say that we made it nearly a dozen feet before I was able to get my balance and bring my team of Clydesdales to a stop. Sherlock snorted with exasperation while Watson looked back at me, no doubt wondering what the holdup was.

Shivering in the cool desert night air (yes, it can get cold in Phoenix during the night), I yawned and looked for the closest patch of grass for the dogs to relieve themselves. However, before I could spot a suitable locale—and also realizing I didn't have any poop bags with me—movement in my peripheral vision had me looking to my left. There, darting stealthily away from me and heading toward the parking lot, was a figure dressed in black and clutching something close to his or her chest.

Having seen weirder sights in my many years of living in Phoenix, I grunted once and turned back to the dogs. I had spotted a designated 'pet area' and was ready to guide the dogs to it when I heard a loud cry of alarm. Then, the door to Vance's casita banged open. He was hastily pulling on clothes when he spotted me.

"Zack? What are you doing up? Did you hear…? Scratch that. Did you see someone run by?"

I nodded. "As a matter of fact, I did. Why?"

Vance hurried out of his casita and hastily stooped to tie the laces on his shoes.

"Where'd he go? Quick, man. We have to find him!"

"He was running toward the parking lot," I reported, growing alarmed. "Why? What's going on?"

Several nearby lights flicked on as hotel guests in other casitas were awakened by our loud exchange. Jillian appeared in the doorway to our casita, holding her cell phone.

"What is it?" she asked. "What's going on?"

"Someone broke into my room!" Vance shouted at her, as he broke into a run. "They've taken the laptop! Come on, Zack. We've got to catch them!"

"I'll call the police!" Jillian called out after us.

The dogs took one look at Vance's retreating form and barked excitedly. They knew something was happening, and they were determined to be involved. Therefore, when I sprinted after my friend, the corgis didn't need to be asked twice. As it turns out, I was the one in danger of being left behind, since it was all I could do to keep up with Vance and the dogs.

We arrived at the parking lot just in time to see a dark, unmarked van go peeling out onto the street. I cursed loudly, and even remembered thinking that I was glad Jillian wasn't there to hear me. Vance then jingled his keys in front of me, as if he knew this might have been a possibility.

I caught sight of our rental van, where Randy had returned it earlier in the evening. However, Vance brushed by me as he ran for the *other* car. I immediately scooped up the dogs and ran as best as I could after him.

"Buckle up, amigo," Vance told me, as the Challenger roared to life. "That son of a bitch is not getting away from us."

I cast an anxious look at the corgis in the back seat, who were each standing up on their hind legs so they could see out the windows. My seatbelt clicked into place and I nodded my readiness. Then, I was slammed back into my seat as all 500+ horses that were hiding under the hood surged to life at the same time.

I will say, for the record, that had I known that's how much horsepower the car possessed, then I probably would never have gotten into the blasted thing with my power-hungry friend. But, that doesn't do me any good at the moment. From Vance's perspective, an important piece of evidence had been stolen, from under his own nose, and my detective friend was determined to rectify the situation.

It felt as though the Challenger burned rubber through the first three gears. We were on E. Camelback Road, traveling west, before I was able to catch my breath. Vance, to his credit, handled the car like a pro. We were weaving in and out of traffic so fast that I actually had to shut my eyes a few times. He delicately shifted through the gears as he navigated around obstacles and not once, I might add, did he touch the brakes. How he managed to keep all four wheels on the ground as we rocketed by other vehicles was beyond me.

And speaking of traffic, what the bloody hell were so many people doing out of bed this early? The sun wasn't due to put in an appearance for just over an hour, yet there was so much traffic on the road that I was reminded of rush hour on the freeway. We were zipping by cars so fast that, to me, they were practically standing still.

Sherlock barked at each car we passed, as though the corgi was scolding the other drivers for being in our way. Watson had lowered herself to a sitting position and was content to keep an eye on things from there. I gave each of the dogs a quick pat before returning my attention to the road. Come to think of it, based on how aggressively Vance was driving, I would have done better sitting in the back seat with the dogs.

"There he is!" Vance cried, as he pointed at a van several hundred feet ahead of us.

The vehicle in question, a dark, unmarked panel van, was traveling erratically across all four lanes as it tried valiantly to shake us from its tail. The van skidded around a slow-moving semi, which caused the driver to slam on his brakes. The semi immediately jack-knifed, and brought traffic to a standstill, but not before Vance zipped by the huge rig just as it slid to a stop.

Then, we watched the van take a hard 90° right

turn. Honestly, I was surprised the driver of the van didn't lose control and roll it. As we neared the turn, I kept expecting to feel the Challenger slow, since I was certain the last thing Vance wanted was to have to explain why he totaled a $50,000 souped-up muscle car. However, what I didn't expect Vance to do was speed up, grip the hand brake, and apply it as he counter-steered around the turn. What was the result? We drifted around the corner, all without having to slow down one bit.

I grinned like an idiot the entire time.

"Dude, where the hell did you learn how to do that?"

"Practice," Vance answered, as he spun the wheel to correct the car. "Lots and lots of practice."

"That's cool as hell!" I exclaimed, as Vance smoothly pulled out of the turn. "You gotta teach me that!"

"You'd need a manual transmission, rear-wheel drive car for that," Vance casually explained, as he shifted through the gears. In a matter of moments, we had caught back up to the van. "Your Jeep wouldn't cut it. It was a dangerous move, and I probably shouldn't have done it."

Just then, we heard the wail of a police siren. A quick check behind us confirmed one of Phoenix's finest was now tailing us. I nervously looked over at Vance.

"They think we are the bad guys here. You need

to tell them that we're on their side!"

"Get my cell. See it on my belt?"

I pulled Vance's cell off its holder and held it out to him.

"Okay, now what?"

"What do you think? Dial 911, and put it on speakerphone."

I did as asked, and when the operator came on the line, Vance identified himself as a police officer from Oregon, and that he was pursuing a suspect.

"I am showing that one of our units is also in pursuit. Can you confirm?"

"It's confirmed," Vance announced, as he raced around a slow-moving dump truck. "Have you been able to verify my credentials?"

"We're checking into that right now. Stand by."

The call was placed on hold.

"What happens next?" I wanted to know. "I mean, once they verify you're a cop, are they going to leave you alone?"

"I'm out of my jurisdiction. While I could argue that I'm obligated as a Peace Officer to intervene, if an arrest were to be made, I would call the local cops as soon as possible. No one wants to encroach on..."

"Detective Samuelson?"

"That's a good sign," I mouthed to Vance.

Vance nodded. "I'm here."

"Your identity has been confirmed. How can we assist you?"

"Would you kindly put me in touch with the unit that's currently following me? And give them a heads-up that I'm a cop."

"One moment, please."

We were put on hold a second time. I couldn't help but notice the van we were pursuing seemed to be taking riskier and riskier moves. It looked as though the driver was getting desperate to shake us, and the last thing any of us wanted was to make him do something foolish.

"This is Unit Charlie-15, Mountain View Precinct. Who is this?"

"Detective Vance Samuelson, Pomme Valley, Oregon. I'm in the white Challenger, in pursuit of a suspect."

"Roger that, Detective. Describe the vehicle you're pursuing. What is the nature of his crime?"

"Theft of incriminating evidence against a large corporation, which more than likely resulted in a murder cover-up."

"Acknowledged. Do you have a make and model on the suspect's vehicle? Where is it now?"

"Late model, dark colored panel van. I'm sorry, I don't have a plate for you."

"Copy that. Is that your van, turning onto Indian School Road?"

"That's it," Vance confirmed, as he stomped on the accelerator. "I'm trying to get close enough to ID the plate."

"Be careful, Oregon," the Phoenix cop warned us. "We're heading into some serious congestion.

I'm not sure how much longer we'll be able to safely pursue."

"Acknowledged. I ... shit. Shit! I lost him! Do you have a visual?"

"Negative, Oregon. There are too many vehicles on the road. I'm afraid we'll have to call this chase off."

"I copy. Dammit! Maybe we can..."

An ear-splitting bark caused us both to practically jump out of our skins.

"What was that? Have you a K-9 unit with you, Oregon?"

I looked back at Sherlock. Both he and Watson were on the driver side of the car, staring out the windows at something on the left side of the road. I couldn't tell what they were looking at, but something had attracted their attention. Had the van pulled off the road, trying to hide from us? Was that why we had lost it?

"Umm, yeah, you could say that," Vance slowly answered. "In fact, I have two of 'em in here, plus their handler."

"Acknowledged. Listen, Oregon, there are simply too many cars on the road. We have to call this off."

Vance down-shifted, bringing the Challenger to a respectable 40 mph. He glanced briefly at the dogs in the rearview mirror and saw that something had attracted their attention. Then he looked over at me with a questioning look on his face, which I nodded affirmatively.

"Listen, man. I know this is gonna sound weird, but I think we both need to pull off the road up here. My dogs have, er, found something. Well, they might be on to something."

"I don't follow, Oregon."

"Actually, do just that. Follow me."

We proceeded to take the first left that we could, which was namely into a Square L convenience store. As soon as we were both parked, we exited the cars. Much to my surprise, not one but two uniformed officers emerged from within the patrol car. The first cop was short, but extremely muscular. He was in his late twenties, had closely cropped black hair, and thankfully, had a smile on his face. The second officer was female, younger still, and had her brown hair pulled up into a tight bun. Vance flipped open his badge as they neared, verified that both saw it, then held out a hand.

"Detective Vance Samuelson, Pomme Valley, Oregon. This is Zack Anderson, police consultant."

"Officer Brad Harding. This is Officer Elizabeth Gutierrez."

We all shook each other's hands. Then, if you're familiar with Sherlock and Watson's history, you'll know what happened next. A black, red, and white head appeared in the Challenger's window and let out a bark of sheer displeasure. Both Phoenix cops glanced over at the car. Officer Harding grunted by way of acknowledgment. But, I did see Officer Gutierrez smile as she saw the dogs.

"Is that a corgi?" she hesitantly asked. "I wasn't aware such a small breed could be utilized as service dogs."

"They're both corgis," I confirmed, "and they are, uh, consultants. Would you come here a second? I have to introduce you two or else Sherlock won't stop his barking."

"Your dog's name is Sherlock?" Officer Harding asked. He finally nodded. "Cute."

As soon as we all neared the car, a second head popped over the window sill. Both dogs panted contentedly as I opened the door. Grabbing their leashes tightly in my own, I lifted each of them to the ground. Vance dropped into a squat and offered the dogs a biscuit.

I stared at the doggie treats with amazement. Did he always travel with a pocketful of those things?

"Sherlock, Watson," Vance formally began, "this is Officer Harding and Officer Gutierrez. Officers, may I present Sherlock and Watson, Pomme Valley's most efficient team of detectives. And yeah, I know how that sounds, being a detective myself. Officers, these two are the reason why we've pulled over. We've lost the van, right? Well, I think these two might be able to find it for us."

"How?" Officer Harding demanded.

"The more I explain, the crazier it'll sound," Vance assured the two local cops. "Instead, I ask for your indulgence as we check out the area."

"That van is long gone," Officer Harding stated,

matter-of-factly. "There is no way your dogs could find it."

"Perhaps not," I added, as I fondly gazed down at my dogs, "but they both suspect something is up. There's something nearby that they want us to check. Can we? Take a look around?"

The two officers shared a look. I couldn't help but think both of them thought we were insane. Vance noticed the look of resolve that was forming on Officer Harding's face. Correctly guessing that he was the senior officer between the two of them, Vance cleared his throat.

"Okay, look. If we strike out, then I'll personally... er, let's see. Zack, help me out here. What could I wager?"

Being the devious SOB that I am, and since I'm always eager to throw my friend under the bus, I grinned as I realized what I could get Vance to do.

"If we strike out," I slowly began, fighting valiantly to keep the glee out of my voice, "then Detective Samuelson here will hereby voluntarily undergo Wilson's Wing Challenge."

Both cops lit up like Christmas trees. Heads were nodding, and just like that, in the blink of an eye, both cops had dropped their objections. Now, for those of you that aren't familiar with Phoenix and some of its more popular customs, the Wilson's Wing Challenge was an infamous food eating contest, where the challenger agreed to down nine wings and then wait nine minutes, all without having anything to drink. Vance, I could see, was nodding nonchalantly, as though he thought it'd be a piece of cake.

What Vance didn't know was that this particular challenge had only been won by two people. Why so few? Well, most sane people would see the words 'ghost chilies' in the description and wisely back away. Ghost chilies, in case you weren't aware, were quite literally some of the hottest peppers on the planet. I believe even India's military had approved the pepper's use in hand grenades.

I kid you not.

Anyway, Vance shrugged off the challenge, the local cops were amused, and I was allowed to give the dogs some slack on their leashes to see where they led us. Almost immediately, Sherlock turned toward N. Browne Ave. and started trotting toward it, like we were out for a Sunday walk. Vance fell into step beside me.

"Okay, pal. Tell me about this challenge. What did I just agree to?"

"Wilson's Wing Challenge consists of some spicy chicken wings," I told him. I glanced behind our procession to see the two Phoenix cops trailing behind us. They were carrying on a hushed conversation among themselves, no doubt questioning the hiring practices of small Oregon towns. "Anyway, the challenge is well known throughout the city, because only two people have ever completed it."

"Only nine wings? What's the catch? How hot

are these things?"

"Do you like spicy food?"

Vance shrugged. "Sure, who doesn't?"

"I mean, really spicy food."

"Sure."

"Really, *really* spicy food."

Vance suddenly groaned. "They've used those super-hot chilies, haven't they?"

"The hottest there are," I agreed. "Ghost chilies."

"That's just great. Thanks, pal. Sherlock and Watson had better come through, or else I'm making you eat those things with me."

Overhearing our conversation, Officer Harding smirked. "That can be arranged."

My smile melted off my face, the same way I was sure my skin would if I so much as touched those ghastly wings. There was no way I was gonna willingly subject myself to that particular horror, so my two dogs had better come to my rescue. Again.

We walked along Browne Ave. for nearly ten minutes before the dogs turned on E. 2nd St. During that time, I got to listen to Vance bitch. Then he bitched some more. A few seconds later, he launched into a full-scale rant about how someone could have known the laptop was in his casita.

"Someone blabbed," Vance was saying. "Someone clearly knew it was there. There's no other possible way that Semzar could've known about it."

I felt a tap on my shoulder. I turned to see the female cop, Officer Gutierrez, looking at me.

"You're not talking about Semzar Pharmaceuticals, are you?"

I nodded. "We are. My wife used to work there, as a sales rep."

"Used to work there?" Officer Harding cautiously asked.

"She passed away," I solemnly answered.

Officer Gutierrez was instantly contrite, "I am sorry for your loss."

"She passed away almost two years ago," I continued. "And we're pretty sure she was murdered to keep something covered up."

"You think Semzar is trying to hide something?" Officer Harding asked. "They are one of the largest businesses in Phoenix. You'd better have irrefutable proof before you even think about going after them. Their legal team has some of the most vicious lawyers I have ever had the misfortune of encountering."

"We do. Er, we did. That's why we need that laptop back. It belonged to his wife. We believe she had discovered something about the drug she was selling."

"So you think Semzar stole it from you?" Officer Gutierrez asked.

"Yep," I agreed. "Somehow, they knew we had it, so they arranged to have it stolen while we were asleep, only my dogs alerted us just after it happened. That's how we were able to tail the guy this far."

Officer Harding's face had hardened and his eyes flashed fire.

"A buddy of mine on the force had an uncle who took medication made at Semzar."

"Had an uncle?" I repeated, concerned.

Harding nodded. "Yeah. He was never right in the head after that. Donny always said there was something wrong with the meds. This laptop you're looking for, will it really prove that Semzar has been up to no good?"

"That's what I'm hoping," I confided to the officer. "My wife was selling some revolutionary new diabetes drug. I think she believed there was something wrong with the drug and had started her own investigation."

"We have to get that laptop back," Vance was saying. "Semzar must be guilty of something. Why else would they go to such lengths to swipe it right from under my own nose?"

"We don't know for sure it was Semzar," I argued. "But, it'd be a damn good guess that it was," I hastily added, after Vance shot me an incredulous look.

Another ten minutes of walking led us straight to a surprising discovery. We were standing before a large instantly recognizable four-story complex. Sherlock and Watson had led us to a museum. An art museum, which explained why I had never stepped foot inside.

I questioningly looked down at the dogs before

looking over at Vance. My detective friend had a dark expression on his face, as though he believed he had already lost the bet. He fired an angry look my way before turning to look at the museum.

"What are we doing here? There's no way the van is parked in there."

"Maybe they have a parking garage somewhere?" I hopefully asked, as I turned to see if the local cops had an opinion.

Elizabeth, the female cop, turned to point north, "The visitor parking lot is one block that way."

I turned to look down at Sherlock, who only had eyes for the museum.

"Maybe the dogs think the suspect is hiding in the museum?"

Both cops were shaking their heads no.

"The museum doesn't open until 10 a.m.," Officer Harding told us. "However, the lobby is open to the public, only all the wings will be closed off with security gates. You won't find our perp in there. There'd be nowhere to hide and nowhere to run."

The dogs pulled on their leashes. They wanted to go inside. I looked at Vance and shrugged. I gave the dogs some slack in their leashes and was guided to the museum's lobby. Bemused, the two local cops followed us in.

"What are we doing here, guys?" I asked the dogs, as I pushed our way through the front doors. At this time of the morning, there was no one in the lobby. "See? There's no one here. There's no place to hide."

Sherlock snorted and led me over to several rows of public storage lockers. Evidently, the museum had a rule which forbade any of their guests from wearing a backpack, or carrying any type of bag. If you happened to have one, then you were expected to utilize one of their free lockers for the duration of your visit. I nodded. It made sense. The last thing the museum wanted was for one of their priceless artifacts to go waltzing through the front door, undetected.

"Are you suggesting the perp stashed the laptop?" I asked, as I gazed down at my dogs. "Come on, guys. That's a long shot, even for you two."

We arrived at the lockers and within moments, Sherlock was sniffing the lower row. He promptly sat in front of one. Watson was a little more selective when it came to deciding which locker she'd like to sit by. And, I noticed she made her choice without checking to see which locker Sherlock had selected. In this case, they each had selected the same one.

"Okay, I'm convinced," Vance was saying. He was reaching for his phone when he remembered that two members of the Phoenix police were already present. "Guys? I think we need to open this locker.'

Officer Harding checked his watch.

"We have a few hours before the museum opens, but I believe we can call a member of the security staff. They should have someone monitoring the grounds at all times. Give me a moment."

It took longer than a moment. In fact, it took nearly a full hour before a representative from the museum's security staff walked through the door. Evidently, the security guards watched the premises from offsite after hours. It was yet another example of the power of the Internet.

"What can I do for you gents?" a middle-aged man with short gray hair asked. He noticed Officer Gutierrez and smiled politely. "And miss. How can I be of service today?"

All four of us pointed wordlessly at the locker both dogs were still sitting by. The security guard looked questioningly at the four of us, as if he was preparing to give us a scripted reason why he wouldn't open it, when Vance pulled out his badge and flashed it to the guard. Then both Phoenix cops also indicated they wanted the locker opened.

The security guard grunted once and pulled out a huge ring of keys. After fishing through various keys, one was singled out, inserted into the lock on the locker, and just like that, the locker opened. Nestled inside, with the power cord still wrapped around it, was Samantha's ultra-sleek laptop.

"I'll be damned," I heard Officer Harding say.

"Well, aren't you two both good doggies?" Officer Gutierrez cooed, as she squatted next to the corgis and stroked their fur.

Sherlock and Watson writhed on the ground in sheer ecstasy.

I started to reach for the laptop when Vance, Harding, and Gutierrez all shouted 'No' at the same time.

"It has to be dusted for prints," Vance explained.

"Then, it's gonna be put back in there," Gutierrez told me. "We're gonna find out who's planning on coming back to pick this thing up."

NINE

O kay, I'll admit it. I was uncomfortable, the vehicle we were sitting in smelled like a gym locker, and my ass had long fallen asleep. However, I was having the time of my life. Why? Because I was part of an honest-to-goodness police stakeout! How cool is that?

Vance, our two new Phoenix friends, and I were sitting inside a dusty, dirty, smelly cargo van parked just outside the museum. Thanks to a discreetly placed webcam, we were able to keep an eye on the locker with the laptop, all without fear of being discovered.

I should also point out that yes, there was a laptop sitting inside the locker, but was it Samantha's? Nope. It had been replaced by another. Neither Vance nor I wanted to risk something happening to that particular computer, so Officer Gutierrez had volunteered the use of her own patrol laptop.

"So, tell me more about this arrangement," Officer Brad Harding was saying. "You aren't a cop, but you are a consultant. You own two dogs, but not a gun. And you're some type of writer?"

I nodded. "That's right. Sounds weird, I know, but it works out fairly well for us."

"And these two dogs have solved a murder before?" Officer Elizabeth Gutierrez asked, doubtfully.

Vance wordlessly held up six fingers.

"Six?" Elizabeth repeated, amazed. She looked down at Sherlock, who was stretched out by her feet, and gave him a scratch behind his ears. "Well, aren't you a smart boy!"

Watson lifted her head and turned her woeful eyes on the female cop.

"Oh, I know you're special, too. For every man, there's always a good woman nearby, to make all the important decisions."

I turned to regard Elizabeth with a grin on my face. Vance and Brad also turned to look, although neither of them were smiling.

"If only Jillian could've heard that comment," I chuckled.

"Who's Jillian?" Elizabeth wanted to know.

"My girlfriend. She's back at the hotel. I had her give Randy the keys to the van so that he could go gallivanting around the city again today."

"I'm sorry, Randy is...?"

"My late wife's brother," I explained. "He's been helping us by leading Semzar on a wild goose chase through the city."

"How?" Brad asked, as he focused his attention

on me.

"We found a tracker on our rental van," Vance explained, as he sat up in his chair and stretched his back.

I pointed at the two dogs, "You mean, they found the tracker, don't you?"

Vance shrugged and returned his attention to the monitor.

"How were they able to do it?" Elizabeth genuinely asked. "How do they know where to look?"

I held my hands up in an 'I haven't the foggiest' gesture.

"So, Mr. Anderson, do you split your time between your writing and consulting for the local police?"

I looked over at Officer Elizabeth Gutierrez and politely shook my head no.

"I wear a couple of different hats. When I'm not a consultant, I'm usually looking after my winery."

"You own a winery, too?" Elizabeth asked. "What's it like to make your own wine? Do you ever become bored?"

There was something about the way she asked the question that had me raising my red flags. Was she openly flirting with me? I quickly glanced down at her hand and saw that her left hand was ringless. Swell. She did hear me refer to Jillian as my girlfriend, didn't she? And, I had to have probably twenty years on her, easy.

"There's way too much to do around the winery to allow me to become bored," I answered. "Besides, being a winery owner isn't my first profession. Writing is."

"He writes romance novels," Vance snorted with amusement.

"A romance writer," I confirmed, holding my head high. I used to shy away from telling people what I do for a living, but lately, thanks to Jillian's encouragement, I've been proud to announce I'm a self-employed writer.

Elizabeth perked up at this.

"Really? Would I have read anything you have written?"

"Only if you're into those sappy love stories," Vance snickered.

"I also write under a pseudonym," I added. "You won't find my personal name on any romance novels, but you will see my nom de plume."

"And what's that name?" Elizabeth wanted to know.

"It's Woolworth something," Vance answered, still grinning merrily away.

"It's Chastity Wadsworth," I answered, giving the young cop a grin. "It's a name I've used for years."

"Chastity Wadsworth? Are you telling me you're the author who wrote *Misty Moors*? That's my favorite book of all time!"

Once again, Vance's smug smile melted off his face. I gave him a victorious grin, which caused him to scowl harder. I stretched back in my chair, interlocked my fingers together, and cupped them behind my head. Vance made sure he wasn't being watched and then flipped me the bird.

"What can I say? It's a living, and one I enjoy making. But, to be honest, I do enjoy keeping the winery running, in my late wife's honor. And, much to my surprise, Lentari Cellars has almost matched my book sales, and if my winemaster has anything to do with…"

I trailed off as I saw that this time, I had Brad's attention.

"Your winery? It's called Lentari Cellars?"

I nodded. "Yep. It was already named when I took over, and I liked the name so much I left it as it was. Why? You couldn't possibly have heard of it, could you?"

"My parents are wine drinkers. They've been harping on me to try their new favorite dessert wine, something called…"

"Holiday Hearth?" I asked, knowing full well the officer was talking about my winery's newest flavor. In fact, it had only been released less than a month ago. How someone in Arizona could possibly know that was beyond me.

Brad snapped his fingers and offered me a grin, "Yeah, that's it. That's your wine?"

"One of the flavors we have, yes," I admitted. "It's actually our newest flavor, and I'll be honest and say that I'm surprised as hell that it's for sale down here."

"It's not. My parents had a small glass of it at

some party they attended last month."

"Was it in Oregon?"

Brad nodded. "Portland."

"I still didn't realize it was for sale anywhere other than Pomme Valley, but I can't say I'm too surprised. Caden is a whiz at the day-to-day operations of the winery. It makes sense he's already selected which retailers will carry the new flavor. Tell you what. If you give me your parents' address, I'll have Caden send them a bottle of it. On me."

Brad's cool exterior evaporated in a flash and suddenly he couldn't shake my hand fast enough.

"Thanks! Thanks so much! Actually, if it's okay with you, I'd like to give you my address instead. That way, I can ... uh, that is to say, I could..."

"Pawn off the bottle as a present from you?" I asked, smiling.

Brad gave me a sheepish smile and slowly nodded.

"That's fine. I'm okay with that."

Brad suddenly sat forward and snapped his fingers.

"Heads up, people. I think we have our guy!"

We all eagerly leaned forward to watch the monitor. What I saw was an ordinary looking guy, wearing a suit and tie, walking steadily, but assuredly, toward the corner of the lobby set aside for the public access lockers. I also couldn't help but notice that not once did he check over his shoulder to see if he was being followed. Significant?

"So, who do we have here?" Brad eagerly asked as he studied the screen. After a few moments, he turned to look over at the two of us. "Do either of you recognize this guy?"

I studied the screen. The figure appeared to be young, perhaps early twenties. I couldn't tell from the video how tall he was, but based on the chairs he walked by, and the counters, I'd say he was much shorter than me. Maybe 5'7"? And, I'd say I had a good 100 lbs. on the guy.

I watched as the suspect finally stopped to stare straight at the camera. I watched his features. Not once did I see a look of concern pass over his face. In fact, the guy strode fearlessly up to the locker, punched in a code on the small keypad, and then opened the locker door. I saw him shift his weight from leg to leg as he remained, mired in place, in front of the locker. Then, the locker door was closed, the guy turned on his heel, and he hurried away.

"How long are we gonna give him before we haul him in?" Vance wanted to know.

Brad continued to watch the screen.

"Right about there will do. Okay, all units, move in! Move in!"

The lobby erupted with police personnel. In a matter of moments, the unknown man was surrounded, had a pair of cuffs slapped on him, and was forcibly shoved into a chair. The bag was slipped off his shoulder and set before the table next to the chair. Brad looked at us and nodded.

"Care to tag along? This is your collar, after all."

Vance nodded. "Absolutely. Thanks. Zack? Do you want to come?"

I eagerly nodded and practically leapt out of my chair. The corgis, who were dozing next to me on the ground, leapt to their feet as well. Gathering up their leashes, I led them out of the van and out into the fresh air.

"I'm gonna have to take a shower when we get back to the hotel," I remarked. "I don't know how often they use that van for stakeouts, but it could clearly benefit from a thorough cleaning."

Vance shrugged. "Was it smelly? I didn't notice."

We entered the lobby and angled toward the lockers. I noticed uniformed guards were stationed every few feet, as though they were afraid the perp would try to make a break for it. But no, there he was, protesting his innocence. He looked younger than even I had guessed, probably no more than a teenager. And, I should note, he was sweating profusely and kept fidgeting in his seat. He looked imploringly at us as we approached.

"Look, man, you gotta tell them to let me go. I haven't done anything wrong!"

Vance grabbed the closest folding chair, spun it around, and then straddled it as he sat down.

"I've got a news flash for you, kid," he slowly began. "That laptop? It was stolen from me early this morning. What do you say to that?"

"I don't know anything about a laptop."

"Well, what do you know?" Brad demanded. "How did you know a laptop was stashed in that locker?"

"I didn't!" the kid insisted. "Look, mister. I'm an intern. I go where I'm told. I also do what I'm told. I don't want any trouble, okay?"

"You do what you're told," I slowly repeated. "All right. Who told you to pick that thing up? Who told you where to find it?"

Beads of sweat were seen trickling down the kid's forehead.

"Look, you can't ask me that. I don't want to get anyone into trouble. I'm just an intern, okay?"

"Yes, you can," Vance argued. "Granted, you may not want to, and I get that. I really do. However, this is a police investigation. Unless you'd like to be charged with aiding and abetting, you will tell us what we want to know. Did you get that?"

I swear, the kid looked like he was close to turning on the waterworks.

"Come on, have a heart," the kid whined. "I just graduated from high school a few months ago. I was lucky to get an internship. If I say anything, I could get reprimanded. Or, worse yet, I could be let go. You wouldn't want that to happen to me, would you?"

The intern looked helplessly from one unfriendly face to the other. He landed on mine, saw that I was holding two leashes, and then dropped his gaze to find two dogs staring up at him. The kid smiled briefly at them before returning his gaze to mine.

"You believe me, don't you, mister? I had nothing to do with the theft of that laptop! I was nowhere near the Phoenician, okay?"

I stiffened with surprise. I hadn't mentioned the name of our hotel. I was also sure Vance hadn't, either. I glanced over at my friend and saw that his eyes had narrowed. He, too, had noticed the intern's gaffe.

"What's your name, kid?" Vance casually inquired.

"Max."

"Uh huh. Got any ID on you, Max?"

"Yeah. In my wallet."

Vance nodded at the closest cop, who happened to be Brad. Officer Harding pulled the intern to his feet, spun him around, and retrieved his wallet. He opened it, eyed Max's driver's license, and then handed it to Vance.

"All right, Max. Let's see what we've got here. Maximillian Rush. Interesting name, kid."

"My parents had a sick sense of humor, all right?"

"Mm-hmm. And what's this? A Semzar Pharmaceuticals employee badge."

"I told you I was an intern, didn't I?"

"Okay, well, here's the problem, Max. No one here has said what hotel this laptop was stolen from, yet you knew it. Plus, you haven't really had a chance to look at the laptop, have you?"

"What's that supposed to mean?"

Officer Harding passed Vance the laptop bag. Vance unzipped the bag, reached inside, and when his hand didn't encounter anything, he thrust his other hand in. After a few moments of fishing around, Vance pulled both hands out of the bag. They were empty. It was right about then that I noticed a cocky grin appear on Max's face. I also noticed the smirk wasn't lost on Vance.

"Go ahead, then," Max sneered. "What's the matter? Didn't find a laptop? That's my mail bag. I do a lot of running for various VPs. I use that bag to hold all their mail."

"Check the locker," Vance ordered, as he turned to the local police. "See if that laptop is still there."

The locker was unlocked with the master key and the door was opened. Sure enough, the laptop was there, right where we left it. A knowing smile passed over Vance's face. He started nodding.

"Very clever, kid."

"I don't know what you're talking about," Max whined. "Go ahead. Dust it for fingerprints. You'll see that I never touched that laptop."

"True," Vance agreed. "I already know you didn't touch it, but then again, you and I both know that isn't the laptop you stole from my room. Why else did you turn tail and haul ass outta here? You knew you had been compromised. 'Fess up, kid. Who hired you to steal that laptop?"

"But I didn't touch that laptop!" Max whined.

Vance reached behind the desk and gently placed the decoy laptop on the desk. After a few moments of silence, Vance handed the laptop to Officer Gutierrez.

"Thank you for the use of your laptop, Officer."

Elizabeth nodded. "My pleasure, Detective."

Max eyed the retreating officer and closed his mouth. He defiantly returned Vance's glare, made sure he was being watched, and then closed his mouth with an audible snap. Vance, however, was having none of it.

"Think you're being clever? We already know you're the one who swiped it in the first place. What's the matter, kid? Semzar doesn't want us to see what's on it? You should have destroyed it when you had the chance. Now, it's going to be used to take down that company."

With a cry of alarm, Max shrugged off Brad's restraining hands, pushed past Vance, and threw himself at the front door, as if he thought he'd be able to escape. On foot. While handcuffed, even. However, he only made it a few steps before Sherlock leapt forward, timing it so that he had jumped between Max's legs, and then slid to a stop. Max landed hard on his knees, eliciting cries of pain as he slammed to a stop a mere two feet from the door.

Before the young intern could move, Brad and two other officers physically yanked Max to his

191

feet and hauled him back to his chair. Clucking his tongue like a disapproving mother, Vance slowly sank back down into his chair opposite Max.

"We can do this the easy way or the hard way," the detective began. "I'll tell you right now that we're really not too interested in the small fish. We want the big ones, namely who was responsible for telling you to steal that laptop. How did you even know I had it?"

Max glared angrily at me and refused to say anything.

"Let me guess. You were watching when our pizza was delivered last night, weren't you? Somehow, you knew that laptop was going to be delivered to us, isn't that right?"

"You still have no proof it was me," Max sneered.

"Sure I do," Vance countered. "I have you. You already told me that you were nowhere near the Phoenician. Since I haven't yet told anyone where we were staying, it wasn't too hard to figure out you were the one who broke into my room."

"I heard the name of the hotel from one of you," Max insisted.

"Too bad that's not true," Vance idly commented. "No one knew, except for Zack here. Oh, and of course, Sherlock and Watson."

Upon hearing their names, both corgis looked up at Vance and gazed expectantly at him. The detective dropped to a crouch, pulled out two doggie biscuits, and fed them to the corgis. Then, grinning, he looked up at Max.

"Now ... are you going to tell me who ordered you to steal that laptop from me, or are you going to go down for murder? It's your choice, kid."

For the first time, Max's resolve seemed to falter. A look of disbelief swept over his features.

"Murder? I haven't murdered anyone! You can't hold me for murder!"

"On the contrary," Vance argued, "the charges we'll be leveling against Semzar Pharmaceuticals will be first degree murder, and conspiracy to commit murder."

"No one's been murdered!" Max cried.

Vance turned to point at me. "Wrong. His wife was murdered, nearly two years ago. She discovered that Semzar had released another dud and, when she reported her findings, your company had her silenced. Permanently."

"There's nothing wrong with any of our products!" Max insisted. "You're wrong!"

"Am I?" Vance snapped. He leaned forward and tapped Samantha's laptop. "Do you have any idea what's on this thing? We do. I went through it last night. It was very, uh, enlightening."

"Impossible," Max breathed. "All company laptops are secured."

"We have her password," Vance smugly countered. He yawned, as though he had become bored of this interrogation. "So, are you ready to come clean? Who sent you to my hotel room?"

"Go to hell," Max mumbled.

"Strike one, pal. I'll try again. Who ordered you to steal this laptop?"

"Bite me," Max growled.

"Strike two. Should there be a third strike, then you will be arrested and taken into custody. Officer Harding, would you care to remind our friend here as to what he'll be charged with?"

"Why, I'd be delighted, Detective Samuelson. Mister Rush, you will be charged ..."

"All right!" Max shrieked, in a voice loud enough to make Officer Harding jump. "All right! I'm not going down for this. I have nothing to hide! I was just following orders!"

"Whose orders?" Vance wanted to know.

"Ms. Lawson."

I paled and felt my face drain of color. "Oh, holy hell. Tell me her first name isn't Abigail."

Max shook his head. "It isn't. It's Maureen. The only thing I know about her is that she's some bigwig's secretary. She's the one who told me I had to retrieve a stolen company laptop and that I might have to sneak into a hotel room to do it."

"Sneak into a hotel room?" Vance repeated, incredulous. "That's called breaking and entering, pal."

"You make it sound like it's a felony," Max sniffed. "It's not."

Vance nodded. "You're right, kid. Burglary is, however. And, since you stole this laptop from my room, congratulations. You're going to become a convicted felon."

"Who does this Ms. Lawson report to?" Officer Harding asked. "Would he, or she, be the one calling the shots?"

We all turned to Max.

"Well?" Vance prompted.

"Mr. Ridley," Max sullenly answered.

"And what does Mr. Ridley do?" Vance wanted to know.

"I don't know. I do know that he's a VP, but of what, I'm not sure. There are way too many VPs to keep tabs on them all."

"Mr. Glenn Ridley," Officer Harding announced, holding her phone. "Their website says that he's the VP of Excellence."

"Corporations," Vance groaned. "Only there will you find messed up titles like, 'Vice President of Excellence'. All right, what does a VP of Excellence even do? What's he responsible for?"

"He's responsible for ensuring process improvement to drive efficiencies, decrease costs, and thereby increase net revenue," Max haughtily answered.

"Does anyone else need help understanding what that means?" Officer Harding asked.

I raised my hand, along with Elizabeth, Vance, and everyone else who had heard the question.

"Okay, translate that, please," Vance ordered.

"Translate?" Max demanded. "That's about as dumbed-down a definition I can come up with. Hmm, how about, he makes things work better so expenses go down and therefore allowing the corporation to keep the profits. If you don't understand that, Detective, then I highly suggest enrolling in night school."

"I thought you didn't know him," Vance accused.

"I don't," Max confirmed. "But I do know what his job entails. Most interns do. It's what we strive to become."

I raised my hand. "Can I ask him a question?"

All eyes turned to me. Vance held out a hand, indicating I should continue.

"How, exactly, did you break into Vance's hotel room? It's not as if you busted a window, or anything. No, you went through the front door. That door is protected by an electronic hotel lock. That means you needed a key to get in."

Surprised, Vance gave me a thumbs up and turned back to Max.

"A very valid question. How *did* you get into my room?"

I do believe ol' Max just turned a few shades whiter, if possible.

"You've gone pale, amigo," Vance dryly commented. "Spill. How'd you make it in?"

"I, uh, used a key."

"What key? There was only one key issued to me when I checked in. Did you somehow get your hands on a housekeeping key?"

Max sullenly shook his head.

"Did you steal a manager's key?" I asked.

Max gave another shake of his head.

"Answer the question, Mister Rush," Officer Harding snapped. "How did you gain access to Detective Samuelson's room?"

"I used a key card," Max quietly answered. His eyes had fallen to the floor and there they stayed.

"Whose key card?" Vance demanded.

"My own."

I blinked with confusion. His own? How was that possible?

"You created your own card key, didn't you?" Officer Gutierrez guessed. When we were all staring at Elizabeth, she continued. "I knew a guy from the academy who had a device that could read the data on those magnetic strips found on cards and encode them onto new cards. I'm guessing you had access to a machine like that, didn't you?"

I looked over at Officer Harding and pointed down at Max's wallet, which was still sitting on the table.

"Yes, Mr. Anderson? Do you have a question?"

"Could you pull his employer badge back out? Would you tell me if it has a magnetic strip on the back of it?"

A quick check of Semzar's badge confirmed that it did have the strip. That meant that the pharmaceutical company had one of those devices Elizabeth had referenced, and were using it to create their employee badges. The question was, who was in control of that machine?

"What do you need to be able to run one of those card-making devices?" Officer Harding asked his junior officer.

Elizabeth shrugged. "Just a computer, actually."

I held my hand up again.

"It's not just the card key," I began, "but the code itself. That machine obviously can make replica cards. However, it needs the source code, doesn't it? How did the operator of that machine get the source code to Vance's door lock when the only key coded to his room never left his possession?"

I have to stop here for a second and gloat. You see, it's not often that I not only ask the million-dollar question, but actually think of it, too. In this case, I had every single person standing around Max staring suspiciously at the intern, wondering the same thing I had just thought of: how was access attained?

"A damn good question, Zack. All right, Max. Spill. How were you able to replicate my card key when Zack was right in that it never left my wallet?"

Was it me, or was Max sweating so much that you would have thought he was sitting under a row of heat lamps?

"Someone hacked into the hotel's computer," Vance guessed. "That's got to be the answer. I'm right, aren't I, Max?"

The intern refused to lift his eyes off the ground.

"What about the operator of this card machine?" I asked. "I can't imagine the user operating the computer running that gadget would willingly create a false card for someone else."

"Who'd have the responsibility of running something like that?" Vance asked. When no one answered, he turned to address the people who were standing nearby, listening. "Anyone? I'm looking for suggestions, people."

Elizabeth raised her hand again.

"You're right. It's about permissions. A machine that can recreate any card with a magnetic strip could be very dangerous if it fell into the wrong hands. Therefore, I would think that only the head of that department would have access to it."

"So, that gives us two suspects," Vance said. He jotted some notes down in his notebook. "I think we need to bring in this Glenn Ridley character and also whoever is heading up their IT department. However, this is your jurisdiction, not mine."

Harding was shaking his head. "No, you're absolutely right. We have nothing to pin him to your vic's murder, but we can certainly bring him in to ask about this break-in."

"We also need to bring in the computer guy," I decided. "Chances are, if he isn't the one who hacked the hotel's computer, then he knows who did."

"Or else gave the order to do it," Vance added. "And yes, you're right, Zack. We need to bring him in, too. We just need to find out who it is."

"That'd be one Arthur Mazlo," I announced, a few moments later.

"And how the hell would you know that?" Vance demanded. "Is there something you're not telling me, buddy?"

I held up my phone. "Nope. Semzar's corporate website has an 'About Us' page. He's listed in there. See? VP of Information Technology. They don't have a photo for him, so we don't know what he looks like. Anyway, he'd be the one to ask."

Vance looked over at the two Phoenix cops who had been tasked with assisting us and pointed at Max.

"Would you care to do the honors?"

Brad Harding's face turned grim and he nodded. "Absolutely. Maximillian Rush, you're under arrest. You have the right to remain silent. You have the right to…"

The dogs and I stepped outside as Max was led away, his head hanging low with shame. As I waited for Vance, who was busy chatting with a few Phoenix police bigwigs, I sent off a message to Jillian, who would undoubtedly be waiting for some word on what was going on.

We caught the guy. He confessed that he was the one who stole the laptop from Vance's room in the first place.

That's wonderful news! About that laptop …

What about it?

Will you be able to bring it back to the hotel?

I think so. Why do you ask?

Based on how badly Semzar wants it back, it must be the key to everything. I'd like to go through it some more.

Shouldn't be a problem.

I used one of the hotel's computers, in the lobby. You should know, every Semzar lawsuit during the last three years has been about glucosoquin.

I'll give Vance a heads up and make sure we bring Sam's laptop back with us.

How soon before you're able to return?

Soon, if I have anything to say about it.

Thank you, Zachary. You're the sweetest!

And don't you forget it.

I had just taken a few steps toward our car when both dogs perked up again. Sherlock started woofing and tugged on his leash, but in a different direction. Curious as to what they were looking at, I gave the dogs some slack and watched as they both headed for the small shopping center across the street. From what I could see, there was a little mom and pop type shop, a smoke shop, a café called Zone, and a small bakery. Looks like they sold a mean donut, 'cause there were tons of people waiting in line in that store.

I reined in the dogs when we hit the sidewalk running parallel to the street. So, what was over there that had attracted their attention? Someone in one of the stores? Perhaps the bakery? What else could the dogs be trying to tell me? I mean, we caught the guy who stole the laptop, didn't we? Hell, we even recovered the blasted thing.

My eyes were drawn to the café. I looked at the word Zone. I seemed to recall seeing the same logo around town, making it a franchise, obviously. Curiosity had me pulling out my cell so I could re-search the company.

There, on my screen, was the answer. It was one of those Internet cafés, the kind where you could rent a computer for as long as you like. Finding an option on their website for 'Locations', I pulled up a map and told it to search for stores in my area. What I saw had me gasping with surprise.

There were stores on 44th Street, several on Camelback Road, two on Indian School Road, one on E. 2nd Street, and several located in Paradise Valley, just to name a few. Do any of those lo-cations sound familiar? Well, they should. Those were the places I've personally visited since I've been back in town. In fact, the dogs have been barking at what I thought were random sites throughout the city. What do you want to bet they were barking at other Zone locations?

The question was, why? Why would they bark at an Internet café? The answer came to me after, for some reason, I spun back around and looked at the museum. Computers. Hacking into hotels. Hacking into cars, for that matter. Those feats required a computer, and over there was a café full of them. Was there something in there that the dogs wanted us to see?

It was time to find out.

TEN

W hat are we looking for?" Vance asked, as soon as we opened the door to the café and strolled inside. Officers Harding and Gutierrez had accompanied us across the street. In fact, I had entrusted Elizabeth to watch over the dogs as Vance, Officer Harding, and I entered the store.

"I'm not sure," I admitted. "I'm hoping we'll know once we see it."

What I saw were several long tables full of computers spaced three or four feet apart. Each station had its own drink holder, swivel arm lamp, and trash receptacle. Of the eighteen possible stations, six were occupied, which I thought strange since it was just after 9 a.m. on a weekday. This place was apparently the place to go if you needed to get online at all hours. I personally didn't know places like this existed. Sure, I knew about Internet cafés, but I didn't realize they were open 24/7. What if someone tried to steal something? Then again, there were video cameras everywhere, with signs posted next to the cameras, stating they were monitored 24/7.

We passed the café part of the shop and noticed it was dark, using one of those separator things to cordon it off from the rest of the shop, much like how a pharmacy would appear in a grocery store if it was closed and the store was not. What was noteworthy was that of the six people present in the café, five took no notice of us. The sixth, however, looked up at us as we entered the shop, emitted a cry of alarm, and hastily grabbed his personal laptop. The young kid slammed it closed, shoved it into a bag, and flung the strap over his shoulder. A split second later, he bolted for the front door.

"Take it easy, kid," Vance called, as he hurried after him. "We just want to talk! This isn't gonna end well for you if you try to run away!"

Apparently, the kid had other plans. He risked a glance behind him, saw that he was being pursued, and doubled his efforts. Thinking he could undoubtedly shake his pursuers in a large, vast building, the kid unwisely bolted across the street and ducked into the art museum, all without bothering to look around. Now, I should mention that the Phoenix police had not yet finished their investigation with the museum. There were cops and museum officials everywhere. Needless to say, it wasn't the kid's brightest move.

By the time we made it across the street, the perp was already in handcuffs. He was led outside and placed in the back of a nearby squad car. Elizabeth handed me back the dogs' leashes and, along with Vance and Officer Harding, approached the car. Since the car's door was still open, the kid watched us walk up to him.

Curious as to why this particular kid fled from us, I watched him closely. As the police started asking questions, I watched the worry on the kid's face morph into sheer terror. What did this kid have to be afraid of? Why did he flee from us? Was he involved with Sam's murder?

It wasn't until one of the cops pulled the kid to his feet, patted him down, and then pulled out the kid's wallet that things got interesting. I watched Vance take possession of the wallet, check the kid's ID, and then, surprised, looked straight at me. I was then motioned over. Gripping the leashes tightly, the three of us joined Vance by the side of the patrol car. Sherlock and Watson, I might add, had become agitated the moment they caught sight of the kid. Within moments, Sherlock was growling.

"You're not gonna believe this, buddy," Vance began. He handed me the kid's ID. It read Charles Etherington. "Chuck here happens to work for a big-name pharmaceuticals company."

I stared at the kid with surprise written all over my face. Sherlock barked twice, as if to say, well, duh!

"Semzar? What are the odds of that? Okay, you might've known it, pal, but the rest of us don't have your sixth sense."

"Why are you talking to that dog as though he can understand you?" the kid wanted to know.

"Because he can," I answered. "What do you think the odds were that we'd stroll in to check that café?"

Chuck scowled and then fell silent.

"Well, Semzar Pharmaceuticals is a big company," Elizabeth informed us. "So, it wouldn't be difficult to figure it out. If we take the total number of..."

The Phoenix police officer trailed off as she noticed her partner's disapproving frown.

"Please continue, Detective Samuelson," Officer Harding urged.

Vance nodded and pulled out a familiar looking card from the kid's wallet.

"You have no right to go through my wallet," the kid fumed.

"Relax, Chuck," Vance soothed. "We just need to ascertain your involvement in this whole mess and why you decided to run. Make yourself comfortable. You're not going anywhere."

"I had nothing to do with it!" Chuck protested. "You can't hold me here!"

"We can, we are, and we will," Officer Harding contradicted.

"One Semzar employee badge," Vance reported, as he rifled through the kid's wallet. He started dropping cards on the trunk of the car. "One Zone monthly access pass. Interesting. One

VIP pass to Chuck E. Cheese. Seriously? What, are you twelve?"

"We need to find out what he does at Semzar," I told Vance. "It might be important."

Elizabeth took Chuck's employee badge and pulled out her phone, "I'm on it."

Chuck, for his part, had started squirming in his seat.

"Gotta go to the bathroom?" Vance casually asked.

Chuck was silent.

"Look, kid. The sooner you come clean, the better it'll be for you."

"I have nothing to say," Chuck stated, as if reading from a prepared statement.

"As you wish. We'll know soon enough. I don't know how, kid, but I do know you're involved. Somehow, you're involved with this cover-up."

"What cover-up?" Chuck asked, as innocently as he could.

"Keep it up, pal," Vance said. Then he pointed down at the two corgis, who had locked eyes on Chuck and hadn't blinked since. "They are the reason I know you're lying."

Chuck looked skeptically down at the dogs before shaking his head.

"You've got it all wrong. I'm a nobody at Semzar. I can't be the person you're looking for."

Officer Gutierrez appeared by our side. She was holding Chuck's employee badge in the air, as though she had found one of Willy Wonka's golden tickets.

"I have an answer. Mr. Etherington here works in IT."

Vance turned back to Chuck and raised an eyebrow.

"Is that a fact? Well, well. You failed to mention that to us, didn't you, pal?"

"Since when is it a crime to work in IT?" Chuck demanded. "I'm not doing anything wrong."

"You sure do keep saying the same thing over and over," I commented.

Chuck sneered, "So?"

"It leads me to believe that you'd really like to think that it's true, only it isn't. So, the question is, what have you done that you know is illegal, but keep trying to tell yourself that it's not?"

"I wouldn't know."

"I can tell you he's a CSR at their IT help desk," Elizabeth offered.

"See?" Chuck cried, as he leapt to his feet. "I'm a … hey!"

Chuck had been forcefully pushed back into the squad car the moment he had stood up.

"I answer phones," Chuck continued. "It's a dead-end job, okay? It's not something I'm proud of. Day in and day out, talking to the dumbest, stupidest people on the face of the planet. Do you have any idea how many times a day I have to tell those morons to reboot their computer? Or how to recover a forgotten password?"

"I'm sensing a wee bit of bitterness there," I

chuckled. "It still doesn't get you off the hook. Why were you running? Would you, perhaps, have a guilty conscience? The question is, about what? Wait a minute. That's why the dogs are growling at you. You must be the one."

"He's the one?" Vance asked. "He's the one who what?"

I pointed a finger at the young kid.

"We just caught the guy who stole the laptop. Then, we learned someone hacked the hotel's computer to get the access codes to Vance's door. And then, we're led over to an Internet café? What do you want to bet he's the one who did the hacking? Why else would he run from us?"

There were two short, affirmative barks. I looked down to see that both dogs had suddenly lost interest in the kid, as if their job was done. Smiling, I nodded. That's what Sherlock had been trying to tell me. The person responsible for hacking the hotel was in that café.

"Is he now?" Vance asked, interested.

Unfortunately, Chuck was no actor. His face became a mask of sheer incredulity as he stared at me.

"No way. There's no way you could possibly know about that."

I pointed at Vance. "Well, he's the one who was staying in the room at the Phoenician. His was the room you hacked. That's how we know about it."

"Oh, shit," Chuck cursed.

"Are you the one who's responsible for re-

motely taking over a car two years ago and causing an accident?" I hotly asked. "An accident
which claimed my wife's life?"

"I don't know anything about that."

"Start talking, kid," Vance ordered. "Spill. If
you don't want to go down for multiple charges,
including murder in the first, then you'd better
tell us all about how you hacked into my hotel's
computer so you could open my door."

"All right!" Chuck cried. "It was me, okay? I was
paid a nice chunk of change to steal an access code
from a Scottsdale hotel. That's all I really know
about it, I swear!"

"Who hired you?" Vance and Officer Harding
asked, at the same time.

"I don't know," Chuck admitted. "He never told
me his name. We've only corresponded via email."

"You're a hacker," I pointed out. "You're telling
me that you didn't try to find out the name of the
person who hired you?"

Chuck's gaze dropped to the floor.

"You did!" Vance exclaimed, delighted. "Beautiful. I'll take that name, please."

Chuck stared, unblinking, at the ground.

"Perhaps you don't fully understand the ser-
iousness of the situation you're presently in,"
Vance said. He pointed at me. "His wife was murdered to cover up something Semzar was doing.
His wife's work laptop surfaces, and is promptly
stolen out of my room, which you had a hand in,
whether you think so or not. You provided access

to my room, which makes you an accessory, get it?"

"Yes," Chuck meekly answered.

"The only chance you're going to get to avoid jail time is with your full cooperation, you got that?" Officer Harding snapped. "And if you refuse in the slightest, then we can only assume you want to spend the next twenty years behind bars. This offer is going once ... going twice..."

Chuck sighed and nodded his head. "Fine. I'll do whatever it takes. I was promised that I would never be caught."

"Who promised you?" I asked. "Who told you to steal that data from the hotel?"

"He never told me his name," Chuck repeated. "As I said, we only ever communicated through email."

"You said you tracked him down, didn't you?" Vance recalled. "What did you find out?"

"Nothing much. A couple of cops drove by the front of the building. I panicked and had to log out."

"How much did you get paid for the job?" Vance asked.

"25K."

"That's a lot of money," I whistled. "How long did it take you to hack the hotel's computer?"

"Please," Chuck scoffed. "Their network uses WPS encryption. A child could break it. It took me less than twenty seconds to penetrate their firewall. Then, since I had the room number, all I had to do was pull up the access code assigned to that room. Piece of cake. Easiest 25 thousand I had ever made."

I rapped my knuckles on the patrol car's door. "Is it? Considering your present circumstances, I'd say it wasn't."

"How did you find me?" Chuck wanted to know. "I took great care to cover my tracks. I used proxy servers, bounced my connection through multiple countries, and even changed remote locations several times. There's just no way you could have tracked me."

I squatted and draped an arm around each of the dogs. Then I tapped Sherlock's nose, which caused the corgi to snort with surprise.

"I'm beginning to think it wouldn't matter where you were hiding. Sherlock here would've found you."

Chuck ruefully looked at the corgi. Sherlock's hackles were raised, and he hadn't stopped growling at the kid. Watson was silent, although she was by her pack mate's side and watched the young hacker like a hawk.

"You obviously know your way around a computer," Vance began. "Who do you know who could hack a car and deliberately cause an accident with it?"

Chuck shrugged. "No one I know, I promise. I'm not into those kinds of things, you follow me? I'm a rule-abiding citizen. I have scruples. You can't believe everything you see in the movies."

Vance shook his head. "Horseshit, kid. You accepted a large sum of money to illegally hack into a hotel's computer system. Your scruples mean nothing. Take him away."

Officers Harding and Gutierrez took a few steps toward Chuck when I held up a hand.

"Wait a sec. Before you do that, I have an idea."

"What idea?" Vance wanted to know.

I pointed at the guy who had broken into the hotel's computer system.

"He's a hacker. He's already admitted it. I say we use him."

"To do what?" Officer Harding asked.

"To track down the person who hired him to hack the hotel," I answered. "Whoever wanted the computer from Vance's room is somehow tied to Sam's death, and that's who we have to catch."

"I told you," Chuck began, sighing exasperatedly. "I wasn't able to find anything. I didn't have a chance. I had to log out."

I pointed back across the street, at the internet café.

"Well, Zone is right over there. You won't need to worry about the cops interrupting you this time. What do you say we allow Chuck here adequate time to track this person down?"

Vance nodded thoughtfully. He looked over at Officer Harding and waited, expectantly, for his permission. Brad held up a hand and pulled out his cell.

"I'd like to let him have at it," our new Arizonan

friend told us, "but for something like this, I have to call it in."

"Do you think he can do it?" Officer Gutierrez asked, coming up close behind me. Her lips pursed together as she frowned at the hacker. "There's no guarantee he'll be able to find anything."

"She's right," Chuck implored. "Trying to unlock a user's identity requires some serious, hardcore coding skills. I'm not ashamed to say that sort of thing is above me."

I looked at Vance, but before I could say anything, I heard a growl. I looked down at the dogs and saw that, for some reason, both had resumed their growling at our data thief. Why? Was Sherlock trying to tell us that Chuck was lying? If so, then that was definitely a new skill I didn't know they had. Canine polygraphs. Was there anything those dogs couldn't do?

"I'll bet he can do it," I announced. I looked over at Vance and shrugged. "Give him some proper motivation and let's see what he can accomplish."

Officer Harding finished his phone call. He strode purposefully back over to us and gave us a thumbs up.

"Chief Wilcox has given his permission and his blessing. Let the kid uncover the identity of his employer."

A look of stubborn resolve appeared on Chuck's face. He purposely crossed his arms over his chest. Officer Harding squatted next to the petulant teenager and smiled patronizingly.

"Here are your choices, son. Either give us the name of the person who hired you, or else you're going down for breaking and entering, burglary, fleeing from law enforcement personnel, handling stolen goods, impeding an ongoing investigation, impeding..."

"All right!" Chuck cried again. "If I do this, then I want amnesty. I want a full pardon!"

Surprised, I looked at Vance, who then turned to look at Brad. We walked away from Chuck and huddled together.

"Is that something you can negotiate?" Vance asked Brad.

Officer Harding shrugged. "The chief says we need to get his cooperation. I just sent him a text, outlining what the kid wants. The chief gave me permission to negotiate, and if this is what the kid wants, then unless I hear otherwise, that is what he'll get."

We returned to the patrol car. Chuck was still sitting in the back seat, cuffed, while Officer Gutierrez stood guard. Harding motioned for his junior partner to help the suspect up. Then he pointed across the street.

"Now's the time to see what you're made of, kid. Either you produce a name, which results in an arrest, or you will be going down for every-thing. As long as you aren't implicated in this mess, other than what we already know, then you'll walk after all this is said and done. How's that for motivation?"

"Effective," Chuck mumbled. "Very well. We have a deal. Get me to a computer."

Ten minutes later, we were back in Zone. Vance and Officer Harding were sitting in chairs directly behind Chuck, while Officer Gutierrez and I waited outside, with the dogs. Yet again, I couldn't help but wonder if Elizabeth was trying to hit on me. She kept looking my way and giggling at practically everything I said.

"I can't believe I'm sitting here with Chastity Wadsworth," Elizabeth was saying. "Your books helped get me through the academy."

"The police academy?" I asked, confused. "If you don't mind me asking, how, exactly, did I accomplish that?"

"It was a lonely time for me," Officer Gutierrez hesitantly began.

Elizabeth coughed nervously and then looked away. If I wasn't too far off the mark, then I'd say Ms. Gutierrez was blushing! Thankfully, before she could continue, I was saved by an unexpected encounter. A loud chattering could be heard, and it was coming from above my head. Damned if it didn't sound like a...

Yep. It was. I wandered out into the parking lot so I could look behind me and up. There, perched on the store's awning, was a roadrunner. I may not be able to tell the markings of one roadrunner versus another, but it sure did look like the same one that has been hanging around the hotel. What was he doing all the way out here?

"You usually don't see those guys venture this far into the city," Elizabeth idly observed, as she, too, watched the brown and white streaked bird. "I wonder what he's doing here."

The roadrunner started up its chattering noise again, and this time, it was louder than before. I couldn't begin to say what it was doing. Signaling others of its kind? Perhaps it's a mating call?

The dogs finally looked up at our feathered intruder. Sherlock cocked his head as he stared at the bird, as though he wasn't sure what he should be seeing. The roadrunner made the chattering noise again, and this time, flew off, out across the parking lot.

"I didn't know they could fly that far," Elizabeth observed.

"That makes two of us," I admitted. "I always thought of them like ostriches."

"Meaning, flightless birds," Elizabeth guessed.

The roadrunner noticed it was being watched, ceased its chattering, and flew down to the ground about half a dozen parking spaces away. We watched it peck a few times on the asphalt. The distant relative of the cuckoo turned to look straight at us. The chattering began again as it watched us. If I didn't know any better, then I'd say it was taunting the dogs.

A quick glance down confirmed both corgis were watching the bird. Then, it stopped pecking at the ground, and instead, started pecking at the car parked in the spot where it was standing. As a result, both dogs pulled on their leashes. They wanted a closer look.

As we casually covered the distance to the roadrunner, which surprisingly held its ground, the car suddenly sped away. I caught the 'For Official Use Only' decal on both the driver's door and the back window, but was unable to tell anything else about it. Elizabeth, I noticed, was busy tapping out a message on her cell phone.

"What's the matter?" I asked. "What are you doing?"

"I took down the license plate number," Elizabeth explained, as she pocketed her phone. "Just in case we wanted to find out who it was."

"You thought that was fishy, too?" I asked.

Elizabeth nodded. "Who would peel away like that from a parking lot? Someone who doesn't want to be seen, that's who."

"Or someone who wasn't expecting to be seen," I added.

Elizabeth frowned. After a few moments, she pulled out her cell once more and placed a call.

"Officer Elizabeth Gutierrez, Mountain View Precinct. I need a records check, please. What's that? No, ma'am. No pending charges. Suspicious vehicle. Yes, ma'am." Elizabeth looked over at me and then covered the phone with her free hand. "I've been put on hold."

I touched my left shoulder. "I thought police officers always wore those radios at their hips, with the microphones clipped up here, near their mouths."

Elizabeth nodded. "They do, and I have before. I personally don't like those things hooked to my shoulder. I do have my radio, though. However, there have been an inordinate amount of calls today, so I'm electing not to tie up one of our frequencies, especially for a suspicious call about... what's that? Yes, ma'am. I'm still here. License plate is Wilson X-ray Wilson 5...5...8...9. Vehicle appears to be a late model Infinity sedan, black, four-door, tinted windows. Thank you, ma'am. Yes, you can put me back on hold."

We wandered back over to the storefront. I looked in to see Vance, Brad, and Chuck in deep conversation with one another. I could only hope they had found something helpful.

"Yes, ma'am," Elizabeth was saying, "I'm still here. I ... what's that? No, I did not know that. Thank you, ma'am."

Elizabeth terminated the call and gave me an incredulous look. She then tapped the window, which drew everyone's attention in the shop, and indicated Brad should join her. Officer Harding shook his head, said something to Vance, and then pointed outside. Vance nodded and headed our way.

"What's up?" he asked, as soon as he exited the café.

"We just discovered we were being watched by someone from Semzar Pharmaceuticals," Elizabeth excitedly reported. "Mr. Anderson and I took a brief walk as his dogs chased after a roadrunner, and that's when we noticed a car speed off. They must have thought their cover had been blown. I managed to get their license plate number and just now confirmed my suspicions."

"We were being tailed by someone from Semzar?" I asked, appalled. "I thought we lost that tracker."

"Is that the tracker you mentioned earlier?" Elizabeth asked, frowning.

"We decided to use it to our advantage," Vance replied, with a grin. "Zack wanted to destroy it, but I thought it a better idea to leave it on the van and have it driven around the city."

Elizabeth grinned. "A wild goose chase. Nice."

"Clearly, we missed one," I glumly reported.

"Not necessarily," Vance said. "Think about it. You see what's directly across the street, don't you? It's the museum. Chuck must have informed his boss where he stashed the laptop when he realized he wouldn't be able to go back for it until later."

"Then why were they watching us?" I asked, confused. "If what you say is true, then they should have been watching the museum. Instead, they were clearly watching the café."

"They were watching the suspect," Elizabeth deduced. "I'm willing to wager they don't care about you guys at all."

"I'll bet they do," I argued. "We have the laptop

now. We've got everything we need in order to file charges, don't we?"

Vance shook his head. "Not yet, we don't. We still don't have a name."

I pointed back inside the café. "How's it goin' in there? Any luck?"

Vance sighed and slid his hands in his pockets. "Well, I will say that I believe Chuck is really trying to learn the identity of his employer. If you'll pardon the pun, he's definitely in some zone, because he's talking to himself, jotting down notes on whatever he can get his hands on, and is moving lightning fast. I have honestly never seen anyone type so fast."

"Faster than Tori?" I asked.

Tori, Vance's wife, was the fastest typist I have ever seen in my life. She told me once that she could type well over 120 words per minute. Once I heard that, I Googled 'Typing Tests', just so that I could time myself. Being a writer, I figured my own speed had to be somewhat similar. Nope. I wasn't even close. Oh, don't get me wrong, I'm a decent typist, with a low error count. But, my paltry 83 wpm didn't come close to touching her record.

"This guy is probably twice as fast as she is," Vance admitted. "And don't you ever repeat that to anyone. Tori is damn proud of her typing, and if she found out someone was faster, then she'd either go insane with jealousy or else drive herself to become that much faster."

I guess there's no need to mention that Tori had to be one of the most competitive people I have ever met. Family game night took on a whole new meaning whenever Vance and Tori attended. Most of the time, Jillian and I would willingly split up our team so that we could separate detective from teacher, or else said detective would end up strangling said teacher.

Movement caught my eye. I looked up to see Brad enthusiastically waving at us. He noticed I was looking, pointed at Chuck, and then pointed at Vance. I nodded.

"I think Chuck has found something," I reported.

Vance turned to look inside.

"Go. We'll be right here."

Vance and Officer Gutierrez walked inside. I saw Vance whip out his notebook and start taking notes. That could only be a good thing, right? After a few minutes, Vance wandered outside.

"Good news, I take it?" I hopefully asked.

Vance nodded. "Yes. Well, yes and no."

"Hit me with the good news first," I decided.

Vance nodded. "Alrighty. First off, Chuck was able to track the sender of his email to a Semzar account, which shouldn't come as a surprise."

"It doesn't," I confirmed.

"Right. Now, that particular account is registered to an IP address belonging to one of Semzar's upper echelons."

"Do we know whose it is?" I asked.

Vance consulted his notebook. "The only bit of information Chuck could glean was a username: almightygridiron."

"Sounds like a unique name," I decided. "I wouldn't think that'd be too difficult to track down."

"You would think and I would think," Vance agreed. "However, Chuck can't find a name to go with that account. He mentioned something to me about what he had discovered so far. Whatever it was, it didn't make sense to me, but I jotted it down anyway. Let's see. Ah. Here it is. He said he discovered over ten different proxy servers at play. Do you know what that means?"

Actually, I did.

"A year ago, I wouldn't have been able to answer that. But, thanks to the Olympics playing on television this year, I know exactly what it is."

A look of surprise etched itself onto my friend's face.

"Okay, pal. Spill. How do you know what it is? No, wait. First, just tell me what it is."

"It's a way to channel Internet traffic through another computer," I carefully answered.

"What does that mean?" Vance asked. "Can you explain that in a way I can understand?"

I nodded. "I can, yeah, only you have to promise not to get mad at me."

"Is this something that's against the law?" Vance suspiciously asked.

"Kinda. Okay, listen. I mentioned the Olympics, remember?"

Vance nodded.

"Good. Now, I know what a proxy server can do because I used one to watch some of the Olympic Games, namely those events the networks deemed unpopular for prime time viewing."

"You're not doing a good job explaining yourself, pal," Vance flatly stated.

"Let me finish. In this day and age, if you want to watch the Olympics live on the Internet, you can, only you have to log in with your cable television provider. Do you follow me?"

Vance nodded. "I think so. The cable networks need to verify you have permission to view the programming, is that it?"

I nodded, pleased, "That's right. Now, what if you want to watch an event, but the networks you subscribe to aren't planning on covering it? What then?"

Vance's mouth opened, then closed.

"You don't," I answered for him. "You have to suck it up and just watch the highlights for that night. But, if you happen to know what you're doing, you can fool the websites."

"Explain that," Vance demanded, growing angry.

"In this case, I wanted to watch something that was streaming live, only my cable subscription prevented me from watching it. So, I logged into a proxy server, which routed my Internet traffic through a foreign computer, thus making it look like I was physically in another place. There-fore..."

I trailed off as I looked at my friend. Much of Vance's scowl had disappeared, but he was still frowning. Mostly.

"Therefore, the website thinks you're in a loca-tion that's allowed to watch the program," Vance finished.

"Right."

"I get it. Zack?"

"Yeah?"

"Don't do that again."

"Sure. Sorry."

Elizabeth tapped us on the shoulder. She pointed inside. We could see Officer Harding had pulled Chuck to his feet and was leading him out-side. We met him at the door.

"We have a little more information," Officer Harding began. "I'm not sure how helpful it'll be, but Chuck here tells me it's worth sharing."

"What is it?" Vance wanted to know.

"Buried inside Semzar's corporate network, I found a table which linked usernames to em-ployee numbers," Chuck excitedly told us. It would appear our hacker did not want to see the inside of a jail cell any time soon and thought he had found his get-out-of-jail-free card. "The user-name 'almightygridiron' was linked to employee number 330."

"330?" Vance repeated, as he turned to me. "As in, 3:30 a.m.? Does that sound familiar to anyone, pal?"

"No, it's a number, not a time," Chuck corrected, overhearing Vance's comment.

My detective friend ignored the hacker and stared at me as a look of disbelief spread across his features.

"I'll be damned. This is our smoking gun, Zack! We should be able to get an arrest warrant now."

"I think we need to talk to Jillian first."

Vance stared at me.

"Why?"

"She says she's pretty sure everything we need is on that laptop. She wants some time to go through it with a fine-tooth comb."

"Then, let's get this thing back to her. I'd say it's time you put all of this behind you, buddy."

ELEVEN

W hat if they don't allow dogs in there?" I asked again, as I craned my neck to look up at the towering structure full of glass and steel. "Look at this place. The floors are marble. The brass looks as though it has just been polished. I don't want to break any protocols or anything by taking Sherlock and Watson in there."

It was the following day, just after 11 a.m. Vance and I, after having returned to the hotel yesterday, had compared notes with Jillian, and sure enough, what she had found was enough to confront some very important people at Semzar. Red had called again that night, or morning, depending how you look at it, and had urged us to hurry, as the board was meeting today to reveal some 'exciting' news. If it had anything to do with glucosoquin becoming available to the general public, then we had better make certain that never happened.

Vance strode to the front door and held it open.

"We're about to confront a huge corporation

to inform them that they have a serious problem with their wonder drug. The last thing anyone will be worrying about is the presence of two dogs in their precious conference room."

I stepped to the side and let Jillian and Watson enter first. Sherlock and I entered next, and Vance brought up the rear. We approached the security station and the lone guard, who looked up from his magazine to watch us approach.

"Can I help you folks?" the guard pleasantly inquired.

Vance stepped forward. "Yes, sir, you may. We're here to meet Mr. Emil Gregory, CEO of Semzar Pharmaceuticals. Rumor has it he's in some type of meeting up on the 10th floor of this building."

The guard's pleasant smile remained plastered on his face, only the rest of his body language told a different story. The guard was concerned. My question was, why? What did he have to fear from us?

The guard nodded. "You'd be correct, sir. Last minute board member meeting. I wouldn't be allowed to disturb them even if the building caught on fire. CEO's orders, sir."

"What are they meeting about?" Vance asked.

The guard shrugged. "I don't know for certain, only it was for some long overdue approval for one of their products."

"Glucosoquin," Jillian quietly breathed.

The guard shrugged again. "It's none of my business, ma'am, so I don't rightly know. For that matter, it's none of yours, either."

Damned if the punk rent-a-cop didn't throw in a sneer at the end of that statement. I frowned and glanced over at Vance, anxious to see how he was going to handle the guard. One thing was for certain: with the news we were about to impart, we were about to ruin someone's day. Vance slowly reached into his inside pocket and pulled out a tri-folded piece of paper. He smoothed it out and waggled it in front of the guard.

"Care to guess what this could be?"

The guard squinted at the paper. "No clue. What is it?"

"It's a search warrant," a new voice stated.

We all turned to look back at the front door. Officers Harding and Gutierrez had just entered the lobby, and were followed by nearly a dozen other policemen. That was when I looked outside the building to see a news van pull in and park.

"Nice idea with the news crew," I whispered to Vance. "That ought to strike some fear with them."

"I didn't call for a news crew," Vance said, shaking his head. "I don't know how they caught wind of this."

"The chief might've let something slip," Officer Harding admitted. "We spent the better part of this morning confirming everything you discovered, Miss Cooper. Our techs went through that laptop with a fine-tooth comb. Everything checks out, I'm sorry to say."

I looked over at Jillian, who sadly nodded. Brad Harding's face became grim as he turned to the guard.

"Step aside. Now."

The guard clasped his hands behind his back and deliberately stepped away from his station. However, I couldn't help but notice the smirk he had on his face. I watched his eyes momentarily flick down to something on his desk. Curious, I stepped forward and leaned over to see the guard's work space. There, sitting next to the phone, was a collection of several ID cards, each with an embedded magnetic strip. Realization dawned. Everything around here was probably operated by those cards. The guard would have to be able to check each floor, so those cards must be what he used whenever he went on his rounds. He therefore knew we wouldn't be able to make it up the elevator without them.

"We're going to be needing those," I decided, as I snatched the cards off the guard's desk.

"Leave those alone!" the guard snapped.

I held the cards out to Officer Harding. "You're gonna want these."

"What are they, access cards?" Brad asked.

"That'd be my guess."

The guard's snarky disposition finally crumbled. "Dude, if you use those cards to get up there, then they're gonna know who let you up there. Seriously, man, you don't want to mess with those people on the 10th. Please, give those back! Find some other way up there, all right?"

"Officer Gutierrez, would you escort our friend outside?" Brad asked, as he turned to Elizabeth. Officer Harding looked back at the guard and his features softened. "If asked, then we'll say we found the cards rather than saying you gave them to us willingly, okay?"

The guard meekly nodded before he was led away.

Brad clapped his hands together. "Oh, I'm so looking forward to this. Okay, guys. Let's do this."

We walked past the guard station and approached a bank of elevators. According to the signs above each elevator, certain floors were serviced by certain elevators. Since we wanted the tenth floor, we needed one of the three elevators on the left.

"Now what?" Brad asked, once we were all standing inside what had to be the cleanest elevator I have ever stepped foot in. "The buttons aren't working and there's no place to swipe one of these cards."

I tapped a black sensor pad above the numbered floor buttons. "Try holding a card up against that thing. A lot of the hotels use those, and I'm pretty sure it's what tells the elevator which floor we have access to."

We hit pay dirt with the third card. With the 10th floor button illuminated, we began to rise.

"What's the plan?" I asked, as I looked over at

Jillian.

Brad held up the search warrant. "We're going to evacuate the entire floor and then look around. Somewhere, somehow, Semzar has hidden their incriminating evidence up there. It's our job to find it."

"I think we should confront the board first," Jillian softly murmured.

"What was that?" Brad asked.

"What was that?" Vance echoed.

"The board," Jillian repeated. "They're meeting today. Our informant indicated they were, and the guard confirmed it. I think we should talk to them first and let them know why we're here. They're here, right? We should take advantage of that."

"Why?" Officer Harding asked.

"It's just a feeling. What if Semzar's board members have no idea that glucosoquin has some rather unpleasant side effects?"

"Unpleasant?" I sputtered, as I turned to Jillian. "That's putting it mildly, my dear."

Jillian took my hand in hers and gave it a reassuring squeeze.

"You know what I mean, Zachary. I just think we should let them know first."

The elevator chimed once and announced our arrival on the 10th floor. The doors slid open, presenting us with ... hmm, I really don't know what to call it. To me, it looked like a large colorized checkerboard attached to the wall. Overlaying that was the corporate logo for Semzar Pharmaceuticals. As odd as it may sound, I had only seen Samantha's place of work one time, and that was for a Christmas party. The offices had been so heavily decorated that nothing I saw now looked familiar. The only thing I remembered was where we'd find the receptionist station.

"Which way?" Vance wanted to know.

For the record, I should point out that the first thing you'd see after stepping off the elevator was a sitting area, with upwards of six or seven armchairs present. At the moment, none of them were occupied. As for the two receptionists Semzar employed, they were located through the doorway, in the next room over. I looked at Vance and pointed to the right.

"That way."

"Is there something I can help you..." the curly-haired blonde woman sitting at the left-hand receptionist desk trailed off as she noticed our procession.

I glanced back to see the police officers lining up behind us, like they would do if they were taking a school photo. I saw Vance nod his head at Officer Harding while holding out the search warrant. Brad took the paper and stepped forward. The search warrant was held up so there could be no mistaking what it was.

"We're here to serve a search warrant for these premises. These officers behind me will be assisting me with my search. Do you have any questions?"

The receptionist stared blankly at the document in Officer Harding's hand. Her confused eyes met his and she blinked a few times. Officer Gutierrez appeared at her side.

"Perhaps it'd be easiest if you wait over by the elevators? There you go."

"Where would the board members have their meeting?" Brad asked, as he turned to me. "I'd really like to catch them with their pants down, so to speak."

I shrugged. "It's been a few years since I've been up here. I know Semzar has the entire floor, and I believe the 9th and the 11th, also. Hey, look. There's some type of meeting happening in there. We should try over there first."

Directly behind the large dual receptionist's desk was a huge bank of windows, all of which overlooked the western part of the Salt River Valley. The vast majority of those windows, we could see, were part of a large room that was presently occupied, with a number of men and women seated around a mammoth fifteen-foot table. There had to be room for at least twenty people at that table, and all seats were occupied. Surprisingly, not one of the occupants had glanced up to look through the windows at us, because at the moment, they were all congratulating one another, giving hearty rounds of cheers, and so on.

This had to be the right place. Besides, both dogs were staring straight at the conference room.

Right on cue, Sherlock and Watson tugged on their leashes. I couldn't help but be thrilled and nervous at the same time. It was finally time to confront Semzar with what we knew. It was time to find out which one of these corporate stooges was responsible for Samantha's death. Was it just one or was everyone in that room involved in the cover-up? Officers Harding and Gutierrez, their faces grim, strode to the closed conference room door and, without bothering to knock, opened it.

"What's the meaning of this?" I heard someone ask. "Who are you people? What are you doing here? This is a closed meeting, thank you very much."

"Which one of you is Mr. Emil Gregory?" Brad asked, as he looked around the room. Nearly two dozen men and women glared angrily back at him. "No one? Zack, come here. You said you've met the guy before. Is he here?"

The dogs and I appeared at the door. I heard several whispered comments about how the dogs weren't supposed to be in the building, but more importantly, I then heard several passing references to that time in the park a few days ago where they played keep-away with Sherlock and Watson. It was as I always said: my dogs were more recognized than I was.

I glanced around the room and was ready to announce that I didn't see Mr. Gregory anywhere when I spotted him sitting at the center of the table opposite the windows. Apparently, he liked his view. Semzar's CEO was staring straight at me and had a frown on his face.

"That's him," I stated, giving Brad a nudge in the right direction. "He's the one wearing the black suit and tie, with the purple handkerchief in his outside pocket."

"Old guy, gray hair, purple snot rag?" Brad asked.

"Yep."

Brad nodded and started walking around the table, toward Semzar's CEO.

"Mr. Gregory, my name is Officer Harding. I am here to serve you with a search warrant. We..."

Emil Gregory angrily punched a button on the telephone and snatched up the receiver.

"Get my lawyers on the phone," the CEO coldly told whoever was on the other end of the phone. "We seem to have a problem here, and I want it resolved. Yesterday."

Brad gently placed the search warrant in front of Emil and stepped away.

"You are familiar with what a search warrant is, right? You do know that we're now legally allowed to search the premises? Any attempt to prevent us from doing our jobs will result in me pressing charges. Against you, if that wasn't made clear."

Emil suddenly smiled and opened his arms, as if he suddenly decided he should be more cooperative.

"But of course, officer. I'm sorry, where are my

manners? Help yourself. You won't find anything here because we have nothing to hide. As a matter of fact, I didn't even know there was an ongoing investigation. Perhaps, if you could tell me what you're looking for, I could help point you in the right direction?"

"Mr. Gregory, is there, perhaps, something you need to tell us?" a new voice asked.

We all turned to see an Asian gentleman slowly push away from the large table and stand up, prompting five other impeccably dressed men and women to do the same. One was another Asian man, one was an Asian woman, two were middle-aged men wearing almost identical brown suits, and the fifth was an elderly woman wearing a jet-black, three-piece business suit, with her white hair in a tight bun. The old woman was the last to stand, and she certainly didn't look happy about seeing us.

"Members of the Board," Emil was saying, "I do apologize for this senseless interruption. Rest assured, we'll have this sorted out in no time at all. I..."

"No, you probably won't," Brad countered. "You six are Semzar Pharmaceuticals' board members? Do you have any idea why we're here? Any of you?"

The six members gave barely perceptible shakes of their heads.

Brad turned to me.

"Zack? I think you should be the one to address

the board."

I nodded and pushed my uneasiness to the side. The corgis and I walked into the room and we stopped at the seats recently vacated by the six board members. Consequently, it was directly opposite Emil Gregory. The CEO's eyes were once more back on me, and yes, he didn't look too pleased to see me. I stood in front of him and held out my right hand.

"I don't think we've been properly introduced."

"You may not remember me," Emil Gregory smoothly replied, "but I remember you, Mr. Wadsworth. What is the meaning of this?"

Wadsworth? Oh, that's right. I had given the name Mike Wadsworth when I had first met Semzar's CEO.

"Actually, it's Anderson. My name is Zachary Anderson. I'm the husband of Samantha Anderson. She was a sales rep for your company for a number of years."

"Samantha Anderson," Emil slowly repeated. He finally nodded as he looked up at me. "I do know of your wife. That is to say, I did. I'm sorry for your loss, Mr. Anderson. What does that have to do with today? And why would you give me a false name when we first met?"

"Because I'm here, looking into Sam's death. I believe someone from your organization had her killed."

There were several gasps, most of which came

from the females present. Sherlock and Watson settled to the ground, but for some reason, kept turning to look at the doorway leading out of the conference room. Was that where employee #330 was? One Mr. Glenn Ridley? It must be.

"That's a very serious accusation, Mr. Anderson," Emil was saying. "I do hope you have some type of evidence to support your claims."

"Before I answer that," I began, "I have a question for the board. Are you guys here for a reason? Would it be because the FDA is getting ready to approve glucosoquin for the general public?"

"We're expecting an announcement at any moment," the elderly woman confirmed. "That's why we're all here. Why would you want to know that?"

"Because glucosoquin is not safe," Vance announced. "Because glucosoquin has killed everyone who has ever stopped taking it."

"Impossible," Emil scoffed. "If that was true, then I would have known about it. We have been waiting years for the FDA's approval, and not once has a single negative side-effect been reported."

I had started shaking my head the moment Emil had begun talking.

"Unfortunately, that's not true. My wife was one of the few sales reps that were allowed to sell that damn drug before it got FDA approval. But, what none of you could have possibly realized, is just how methodical my wife truly was. According to her files, she placed follow-up calls to her customers, asking how things were going. Do you know what she found?"

"Oh, do enlighten us," a male voice sneered, from somewhere on my left.

"Who spoke?" I demanded. "Reveal yourself, Mr. Charming."

One could've heard a pin drop in that vast room. Almost immediately, I heard a warning woof. I looked down to see Sherlock staring at a big bald guy five seats away on my left. I felt my temper flare.

"Was it you? Come on, Mr. Clean, don't go bashful on me now. You think I'm making all of this crap up?"

The bald dude defiantly rose to his feet. Damn, this guy was taller than me and had to have at least forty pounds on me.

"Of course you are," Baldy began. "You're just some doof who thinks he has a grudge against our company, and is trying to smear Semzar's good name."

"Did you know," I said, raising my voice so that I could be heard throughout the room, "that for all intents and purposes, glucosoquin does exactly what it's supposed to do?"

"Of course it does," Emil snapped. "Isn't that the point?"

"How about what happens to you should you elect to stop taking your wonder drug?" Vance asked. He appeared by my side and plunked a thick folder down in front of the CEO. "Glucosoquin has the unfortunate side effect of placing the user into a coma within 24 hours after being taken off the drug."

"Impossible," Emil Gregory scoffed. "Do you think we wouldn't have done extensive testing for potential side effects? Rest assured, as far as glucosoquin is concerned, there are none. It's perfectly safe."

"Sadly, that's not true," Jillian told the CEO, as gently as she could. "I found records of follow-up calls Zachary's wife made several months after a sale was finalized, just so she could see for herself how everything was going. Now, I will admit that there weren't many clinics who took their patients off the drug, but for those who did, every single one of them slipped into a coma within 24 hours. Those who didn't receive prompt medical attention passed away less than 24 hours later."

"If that were true," Emil began, "then why have none of us heard anything about this?"

"Clearly, one of you has," Vance countered. "One of you took extreme measures to make sure the public never knew what glucosoquin was capable of."

Semzar's top executive crossed his arms over his chest. "And may I assume you think I was the one responsible for making sure such negative publicity never saw the light of day?"

"Only if you're employee number 330," Vance answered. "Are you?"

This caught the CEO off guard. He blinked a few

times before shaking his head.

"My employee number? No, my number is 14."

"Why wouldn't it be '1'?" I interrupted. "You're the boss, right? Shouldn't you be the first on the list?"

"My Semzar ID number is irrelevant," Emil sighed, his voice heavy with exasperation. "The number is assigned by order in which the employee is hired. However, I will admit I'm now curious about employee number 330. Does anyone know who that is?"

Officer Harding cleared his throat and raised a hand. "We do. But, before we announce who it is, would that person, if you're here, care to identify themselves?"

Much to my surprise, Mr. Clean stepped forward.

"My employee number is 330, and I have no idea what any of this is about. I couldn't possibly be the one you're looking for."

"For the record, will you state your name, sir?" Officer Harding asked, as he turned his attention to the Semzar executive.

"Glenn Ridley. I'm the VP of Excellence."

"Corporations and all their blasted titles," Vance softly grumbled, shaking his head.

Brad reached into a large paper bag and withdrew Samantha's laptop.

"All right, Mr. Ridley, do you recognize this?"

Glenn stared at the laptop and shrugged. "It's one of our laptops, no doubt about it. We use about five different models here at Semzar. I don't know who was assigned to use that particular model. It isn't one of the more widely-used models, if that's what you're wondering. I think that might be the model sales uses."

Brad gave the laptop a slight shake. "No, I'm talking about this specific laptop. This one, right here. Does anyone recognize who it belonged to?"

I quickly glanced around the room, intent on seeing whether a look of recognition would give anyone away. Unfortunately, not one person gave me the slightest indication they had seen that particular laptop before, and that included Mr. Clean, er, Glenn Ridley. So much for that theory. He had to be lying.

"Does 'almightygridiron' have any special meaning for you?" Officer Harding asked, as he focused his attention on Glenn.

"That's one of the usernames I've used on the Internet," Glenn slowly admitted. "How could you possibly know that?"

"That particular username has been linked to a recent burglary at a Scottsdale hotel," Brad answered. "This laptop was stolen from the Phoenician. We believe someone here was getting worried about what we'd find on this thing. That person then arranged to have the door codes from Detective Samuelson's hotel room transferred to a custom-built door card and presto, we have the ingredients for a high-tech robbery. Only, our perp didn't count on having two canine detectives on the case. They were able to alert their owner and follow them to the Phoenix Art Museum, where this laptop was stashed."

"Please," Glenn scoffed. "You'd have us believe mere dogs did that?"

Brad pointed down at Sherlock and Watson. "Yep. If I hadn't seen it with my own eyes, then I would be just as skeptical as you are. As it is, they … Zack? Why do your dogs keep staring at the door?"

I shrugged. "I'm not sure. Someone is probably having lunch out there, and the dogs can smell it."

"Anyway," Brad continued, as he turned back to the big bald dude, "we apprehended the guy responsible for hacking into the hotel's computer to steal door access codes. He has identified his employer as you, Mr. Ridley."

Mouths dropped open as heads slowly swiveled until everyone was staring, aghast, at the VP of Excellence. Glenn held up both hands in mock surrender and vehemently shook his head.

"Hey, I don't know where you get your information, but you've got the wrong guy. I had nothing to do with that. I don't know anything about a laptop robbery."

"What was a Semzar Pharmaceuticals computer doing at a hotel in Scottsdale?" Emil Gregory suddenly asked, frowning. Consequently, the room fell silent. "Those laptops are property of Semzar, and, due to the confidential information they contain, should never have left this building."

"Wait a moment," another voice interjected. "A computer hacker identified Mr. Ridley as his employer?"

We all turned to look as a new speaker pushed his way into the room from the hall outside. He was a somewhat short, pudgy, middle-aged man with long, thinning hair and a full, bushy beard. Unlike the others, he wasn't dressed in full business attire, but rather a simple pair of khakis and a green Polo shirt.

"And you are, sir?" Brad asked, as he turned his attention to the bearded man.

Sherlock jumped to his feet and sounded a warning woof, which caused Vance, Jillian, and me to stare down at the corgi. Why would he bark at this guy? Were we looking at another person who'd be implicated in Sam's death?

"Arthur Mazlo, but you can call me Art. Or Maz, your choice."

"And what role do you have here at Semzar, Mr. Mazlo?" Brad wanted to know.

"Arthur Mazlo is our vice president of information technology," Emil answered for him.

A chill swept over me as I studied Arthur's face. This guy? He was the VP of IT? Hadn't this particular person been mentioned once or twice as a possible suspect? If he was head of IT, then that meant he was in control of the create-your-own-magnetic-card machine. Did that mean this guy also had the skills to hack a car's computer and force it off the road? Could this be why Sherlock was suddenly paying attention to him?

I clenched my fists and gritted my teeth. I had to know if this pathetic excuse of a human being was, in fact, Sam's killer. I studied the pale, overweight man who, I might add, looked as though he rarely stepped outdoors, when a firm, but friendly, hand appeared on my shoulder and prevented me from taking a step.

"Not yet, pal," Vance softly murmured. "Let's see how this plays out first."

"How nice to make your acquaintance," Brad said, smiling, as he and several other officers appeared at Arthur Mazlo's side. "We've been looking forward to meeting you, Maz."

Arthur Mazlo's eyes widened with shock. "Why? I don't have anything to do with this, either."

"Yes or no, Mr. Mazlo," Brad started, as he slid the laptop back into the oversized bag it had come from and withdrew Chuck the Hacker's Semzar employee ID badge. "Do you have access to the machine that makes these things?"

"We do have an RFID dual-sided card encoder, if that's what you're wondering," Arthur confirmed. "So what? Many companies do. Anyone can purchase one. For crying out loud, we bought ours off the Internet."

"And who runs that machine?"

"Uh, well, I do."

"Mm-hmm. What about hacking into a car's onboard computer?"

Arthur shrugged. "Sure. Today's cars don't really have any type of protection in place, so it wouldn't take much to do it."

"Could you take over the car's controls and make it do what you want it to do?" Brad continued.

Arthur shrugged again, oblivious to the hole he was digging for himself. "It all depends on the car. If the car has advanced features, like those designed to help you parallel park, then I suppose you could."

"Arthur, stop talking," Emil snapped. "They're setting you up."

Arthur's eyes widened with alarm and he suddenly raised both hands, as though he were being held at gunpoint. "Hey, now wait a minute. I didn't hack into anyone's car, okay?"

"Yet, you know how to do it," Brad said, as he turned to look at the group of officers standing silently near the doorway to the conference room.

One of them, an older fellow, with more decorations on his uniform than the others, nodded. I narrowed my eyes as I studied the guy. Who was he, Brad's superior?

Officer Harding opened the thick folder he had dropped on the table and pulled out a copy of the police report back from that fateful day.

"Do any of you happen to know how Samantha Anderson died? Her Audi veered off the road and directly into an oncoming semi-truck, killing her instantly. Does anyone else find that incredibly suspicious?"

Gasps and muted whispers were bandied about.

"How could you possibly know that?" Glenn Ridley asked. "I remember reading about that wreck. There was nothing left to examine."

Every single person in the conference room, which included the police, was now suddenly staring at Semzar Pharmaceuticals' VP of Excellence.

"Hey, I know how that makes me look, all right? I knew Samantha. She was my friend. You've gotta believe me, I had nothing to do with any of this."

I started walking around the table, intent on telling Mr. Clean what I really thought of him, when I felt the dogs' leashes go taut. Surprised, I glanced down at Sherlock and Watson, only they were nowhere to be seen. The leash was stretched back the way I had come, and based on how long I knew the leash to be, both corgis more than likely hadn't budged an inch from where they originally sat.

"Guys? What are you doing? Come here."

Nothing. As I slowly walked back to the dogs, I could see that Sherlock and Watson were still staring at the doorway, as though they were trying to see who was outside. Sherlock, I should also add, kept turning to look at Emil Gregory, as if he was afraid he'd try to escape.

So, who was out in the hallway? I couldn't see anyone, but then again, that could be because the doorway was blocked by people. It couldn't hurt to check who was out there.

"Could you guys step out of the way for just a second?" I asked, using the politest voice I could muster.

Three police officers, including the decorated officer I was guessing was Brad's boss, and one guy in a navy-blue suit, slowly stepped to the side. Through the doorway, I could see only one person moving about, and that person was a short, older woman carrying an armful of papers. She was throwing anxious looks into the conference room every time she passed by. Noticing that she was being watched, the woman hurriedly dropped her head and scurried off.

"Who's that?" I asked, as I turned around.

"My secretary," Glenn Ridley answered. "Why?"

I looked down at the dogs. Both Sherlock and Watson had risen to their feet the moment the woman had disappeared from sight. If I didn't know any better, I'd say they wanted to go after her.

Something didn't add up here.

"What's going on, buddy?" Vance quietly asked, as he appeared at my side.

"The dogs have been staring out there ever since we stepped foot in here," I whispered. "There's something about that lady. Could we get her to come in here?"

Overhearing the muted conversation, Emil Gregory was already rising to his feet.

"Glenn? Please ask your secretary to join us."

Glenn made eye contact with the guy wearing the blue suit. He nodded and stepped outside, only to return a few moments later leading the middle-aged woman by the arm. Clearly, Glenn's secretary hadn't made it far. Had she been eavesdropping? And if she was, why?

"Thanks for joining us, Ms. Lawson," Glenn said, as his secretary fidgeted uncomfortably just inside the doorway. "I think these gentlemen have some questions for you."

Vance looked over at me and gave me a blank look. I shrugged. I wasn't too sure what to ask this woman, either. What was I supposed to do, ask her why my two corgis wouldn't stop staring at her? However, before I could say anything, the woman burst into tears.

Several of Semzar's executives hastily vacated their chairs and offered them to Glenn's secretary, who reluctantly sat. One guy handed her his handkerchief while another slid a bottle of water over. After a few moments, the woman looked up.

"Is there something you need to tell us?" Brad gently asked. "Do you have something you need to get off your chest? Why don't you start with your name, okay? Who are you?"

"Maureen ... Maureen Lawson."

"Any relation to Abigail Lawson?" I quietly mouthed. Vance and Jillian both elbowed me in the gut.

"Ms. Lawson, I noticed that you kept passing by this conference room. Have you been eavesdropping on us?"

"Er..."

"I'll take that as a yes," Brad decided, as he again glanced over at the decorated officer. "What..."

"I ... I was just trying to protect the company," Maureen sobbed.

Emil Gregory sank back down in his seat and groaned. "What have you done? Are you saying there are some truths to these accusations?"

The two corgis were switching their gazes between Emil Gregory and the secretary. I should also point out that they were no longer trying to see out the doorway.

"I just didn't want anyone to go through what I went through with Harrison," Maureen sobbed.

I glanced over at Vance and then Jillian, who both shrugged. Jillian held a finger to her lips and then inclined her head toward the secretary. She wanted to hear what the secretary had to say, too.

"What are you talking about, Ms. Lawson?" Officer Harding gently asked. "Who is Harrison?"

"He was my husband. He died from complications stemming from diabetes several years ago."

Glenn Ridley was nodding. "I remember you telling me about him. You were in mourning for quite a while, if memory serves. I gave you time off, Maureen. We were more than..."

"Let her speak," Mr. Gregory ordered, silencing Glenn in mid-sentence. "I repeat, Ms. Lawson, what did you do? Did you actually have something to do with the death of Mr. Anderson's wife?"

"No!" Maureen exclaimed, horrified. "Of course not!"

"Then, what did you do, Mrs. Lawson?" Brad asked, confused.

When the secretary burst into tears, Emil stepped forward.

"You've concealed evidence which corroborates these assertions, haven't you?"

All eyes turned to the harmless-looking, grandmotherly-type woman sitting before us.

"You all have no idea what I've done to insure everyone still has a job," Maureen continued, addressing the startled onlookers. Her sobbing had stopped and now, if I wasn't too far off the mark, it sounded as though she was growing angry. "If it wasn't for me, this company would have bankrupted itself years ago."

A cold feeling of emptiness washed over me. I shrugged off Vance's restraining hand and stepped in front of Glenn's secretary. Maureen Lawson defiantly met my eyes.

"You? Are you responsible for Samantha's death?"

Maureen slowly shook her head. "I have no idea who, or what, you're talking about. This was about making certain glucosoquin would see the light of day so others wouldn't suffer the way I have suffered."

"Glucosoquin is way too dangerous to be approved for the public," Vance argued.

"Don't you understand?" Maureen all but cried out. "They found the cure to diabetes! It's worth the price we've paid."

Before I knew what I was doing, my right hand snapped closed, forming a fist, and my arm cocked back. Thankfully, before I could deliver the punch that I clearly wanted to throw, another arm hooked itself through my own and locked it into place. I turned to look into Vance's surprised eyes.

"She's not worth it, pal," my friend quietly told me.

"By what right have you tampered with glucosoquin's test results?" Emil raged on. "Do you have any idea what you've done to this company?"

"I haven't tampered with anything," Maureen snapped, lifting her nose into the air. "I just made sure certain reports never saw the light of day."

It was so quiet in that conference room that you could have heard a pin drop.

"How?" Glenn asked. "How were you able to read those reports? Your computer doesn't have access to them."

"But yours does," Maureen shot back. "You want to know how I did it? Fine. It was easy. I just pretended I was you, Mr. Ridley. I have everything of yours: usernames, passwords, server access, and most importantly, security clearance. You're away from your desk so often that I could examine those test results at my leisure."

"I have to travel a lot," Glenn weakly protested.

"You knew their drug was killing people, and you were okay with it?" I accused. "How do you even look in the mirror each morning?"

"Glucosoquin is only dangerous if you stop taking it," Maureen haughtily informed me. "That was the first report that I concealed. Let the decision to stop taking the drug be up to the patient. It's a small price to pay, when you never have to worry about diabetes again. As for the other reports, well, the side effects of glucosoquin were starting to add up. Obviously, I had to hide those, too."

"You hid the reports?" Arthur asked, sounding impressed. "Where? On our network?"

Maureen nodded. "They're buried in a hidden folder in Mr. Ridley's personal files."

With a smirk, Arthur produced a tablet and began tapping the screen. After a few moments, he grunted and held the tablet up for all to see.

"Found 'em, unfortunately. She ... whew! She wasn't kidding. I'm sorry, Mr. Gregory, but there are all kinds of reports in here, dating back from about five years ago. I don't get it. Why not just delete them?"

"You found that awfully quick," I quietly observed. However, the conference room had gone deathly quiet, allowing everyone present to hear my comment.

"What was that?" Arthur asked, as he looked my way.

"You found those reports in, what, less than ten seconds? How did you do that? Did you get an anonymous tip?"

Arthur Mazlo's mouth opened, but nothing came out. I then noticed that he quickly looked over at Emil Gregory before dropping his eyes to the floor. There was no denying what I saw. The CEO was scowling at his head of IT. Then, Emil's face cleared, as if a switch had been flipped. The smug smile was back.

Then it clicked.

These two were in it together. That is to say, they were in ... what's the word? Cahoots? Arthur must have directed all damaging reports on glucosoquin straight to Glenn Ridley, knowing full well that his accounts were being accessed by Maureen the secretary. It'd be easy for him, being VP of IT. He'd be able to monitor the flow of information through their own intranet, so it was just a matter of deciding who would be the recipient of all those damaging reports.

Semzar's bigwigs were setting Maureen up to be the scapegoat should any of this ever come to light. Vance must have come to the same conclusion, as he suddenly nodded his head.

"Ms. Lawson?" Emil's voice suddenly said, snapping me back to reality.

Everyone turned to look at Emil Gregory. He was regarding the secretary with a cold expression. However, damned if he didn't have a little bit of a smirk on his face. Now Arthur did, too.

"You're fired."

Officer Harding pulled out his cuffs. Maureen Lawson cringed, but held her ground. That's when I decided I couldn't let either of these two to get away with this scheme.

"Wait a moment," I interjected, as I stared at the woman I was supposed to believe was responsible for Samantha's death. "She's the one who hacked Sam's car? Does it look like she has connections that could pull it off? No. I don't buy it. However, I do buy one of those two arranging it."

"What about Samantha Anderson?" Brad asked, as he turned to look at both the CEO and Semzar's head of technology before looking back at Maureen Lawson. "What happened to her car?"

"I told you," the secretary huffed, "I had nothing to do with hacking a car. I wouldn't have any idea how to pull something like that off."

"I believe you," I quietly stated.

"Then who does?" Officer Harding asked.

"Him," I answered, and pointed at Arthur Mazlo. For the record, both Sherlock and Watson were still alternating their gazes between the CEO and the VP of IT.

"I told you," Arthur began, "I had nothing to do with it. I've never hacked a car before, let alone disabled its brakes."

Vance was suddenly grinning, like a Cheshire cat.

"Who said anything about disabling the brakes?"

Arthur absent-mindedly twisted several strands of his beard and his eyes darted about. "Er, you did, obviously."

"But I didn't," I confirmed. "I only said Sam was in a car accident. I never said anything about the brakes."

"But ... but..."

Ol' Maz had started sputtering and had turned as pale as a ghost.

"So, it's you," I said, as I gazed at the out-of-shape bearded nerd. Vance and I converged on Semzar's head of IT, who had started backing away from us. However, there was nowhere to go.

"You hacked my wife's car and made her drive into the path of an oncoming semi," I accused, as blind hatred washed over me.

The room fell silent. All conversation came to an abrupt halt. Everyone gazed with pity at the wretched simp before me.

"It wasn't my idea!" Maz cried. He immediately swung his gaze around so that he was staring at his boss. "It was his! He said there was a sales rep that would've cost the company billions of dollars if we didn't get rid of her. He said she would've bankrupted us!"

"Don't try to avoid taking responsibility for your actions, Arthur," Emil calmly told his unfortunate employee. "You clearly slipped up. Besides, don't think you can try to pin this on me."

"I can and I will," Maz contradicted. "Do you really think I wouldn't have protected myself? I saved every correspondence and recorded every conversation we ever had, Mr. Gregory. I can promise you one thing: I won't be going down for this by myself."

Emil's smooth countenance finally slipped, and his true feelings finally came through. What I saw had me taking a few steps back from him. A wild, maniacal expression appeared on the CEO's face and he snarled at Arthur.

"Keep your idiotic trap shut!"

EPILOGUE

I t's over. I can't believe it's finally over. Samantha would be so proud of you, Zachary."

We were inside the Masters' home several days later, killing some time before we all had to head back to the airport. With Maureen Lawson's full confession behind us, and Arthur Mazlo's wide variety of proof that Emil Gregory was the mastermind behind the whole affair, it was finally time to go home. Quite frankly, I was glad. It was funny. I used to enjoy city life. I enjoyed the hustle and bustle, and all the activity Phoenix had to offer. Now, the city gave me nothing but a headache. Traffic, houses crammed too close together, lack of open spaces, and tons of people that did nothing but get on my nerves.

Vance, Jillian and I were all sitting on the couch in the Masters' living room, while Jason and Denise claimed the loveseat. Randy had also stopped by, taking the armchair directly opposite his parents. Both Sherlock and Watson were sitting in front of Randy, but that was only because Sam's brother kept feeding them doggie biscuits from some hidden pocket.

"They almost got away with it," Denise was saying. "And that poor Maureen woman. I just don't understand why she would do what she did."

"She lost her husband to diabetes," Jillian told her. "In some twisted part of her brain, she thought people were better off not having to worry about diabetes at all. She just never anticipated any of them intentionally quitting the drug."

"Did you ever find out who had been calling you every day at 3:30 a.m.?" Jason asked. "The woman who claimed she was Samantha's friend?"

I nodded. "Turns out she *was* Samantha's friend, only she wasn't as close a friend as she had implied. Her name was Isabelle Anton. She claimed that she and I had met before, and I'm inclined to believe her..."

"Yet you still don't remember her?" Jillian guessed, after I trailed off.

"Correct. As for the phone calls at 3:30 a.m., well, she couldn't come straight out and tell me she believed employee #330 was guilty, 'cause she also believed she was being watched. She..."

"Who *was* employee 330?" Randy interrupted.

"A VP by the name of Glenn Ridley, only he was just as innocent as everyone else," I explained. "The funny thing is, Semzar's CEO, Emil Gregory, was the one behind everything. He ordered his head of IT to conceal all of glucosoquin's negative side effects. Consequently, Emil Gregory was told of Harrison Lawson's death due to diabetes and played on that."

Jason was nodding. "So, he was feeding the data to that Glenn Ridley person, knowing full well that it was being intercepted by his secretary? And she's the one who arranged to have everything hidden?"

Vance shook his head. "You're close. Mr. Gregory instructed Arthur Mazlo to channel all glucosoquin's damaging reports through Glenn Ridley's account, knowing his secretary had full access to his computer."

"Why?" Denise asked. "Why would that woman go through all of that? It sounds like a lot of work."

"She lost her husband to diabetes," Jillian reminded her. "She truly thought she was doing the world a favor by making sure glucosoquin was readily available to whomever wanted it."

"As for Isabelle," I added, "well, she was just doing what she thought was best. She was right about one thing, though."

"What's that?" Randy wanted to know.

"She was being watched," Vance reported, flipping through his notebook. "Arthur Mazlo knew that Samantha's laptop hadn't turned up. He admitted he arranged to have tracking software installed on practically all Semzar computers, looking for any mention of Sam's laptop. That's how he was able to zero in on her."

"What will happen to the drug now?" Jason asked.

"The FDA had literally just given it their approval," Vance answered, "but as soon as they learned of what had happened, and all those negative reports finally saw the light of day, they revoked that approval and banned the drug. That happened first thing this morning."

"What about Samantha's car?" Jason asked. "Did they ever reveal who was responsible for taking it over? Was it Arthur Mazlo?"

Vance nodded. "I heard back from the Phoenix police chief. Mazlo could have done it, but he didn't want someone's death on his hands. Therefore, he looked for someone else with the skills to pull it off. As it happened, he didn't have to look far. Turns out there was a decent hacker already on Semzar's payroll, and he was fed up with his ... how did he put it ... mundane position at the company. Ring any bells?"

I perked up. "It sounds vaguely familiar. I just don't remember from where."

Vance was nodding. "Right. Wait until you hear where you remember him from. He..."

"Were they able to pick him up?" Jillian asked.

Vance grinned and then shook his head. "No, and that's because they didn't have to. They already had him in custody. Zack, do you remember Chuck?"

I snapped my fingers. "The guy we found in Zone? The one who hacked the hotel to get the codes for your hotel room door?"

"That's the one. Also, in the mother of all twists, it turns out Chuck is Maureen's nephew, although neither knew the other was involved. As for Chuck, he admitted he was tired of answering phone calls day in and day out. He wanted something bigger, juicier. So, when an anonymous email appeared in his inbox, promising a cool 25 grand for what promised to be just a few hours of work, he jumped on it."

"Chuck," I scowled, shaking my head. "All those Zone stores that the dogs were barking at? What do you want to bet that Chuck was at each one, trying to hide his tracks?"

"He's the one who installed the malware, looking for Sam's laptop," Randy guessed.

I nodded. "Right. Do you want to know what's been bugging me? Why did the dogs react to those people in the hotel? They couldn't have been growling at Isabelle, right?"

In response, Jillian pulled out her phone and accessed her photos. After a few moments, she handed me her phone. On the display was one of the pictures she had taken of the group of Semzar employees as they passed by.

"I've seen this before," I told her, shrugging. "What about it?"

"Look closer," my girlfriend urged. "Who do you see there, in the back?"

I held the phone closer. I'll be damned. It was Maureen! She was standing just behind Mr. Clean.

Er, make that Glenn Ridley.

"Those are some smart dogs," I once again muttered, handing Jillian's phone back to her.

"What do you think will happen to Semzar Pharmaceuticals?" Jillian asked me, as she slid her phone back into her purse.

I shook my head. "I don't really know. They have such a history of creating pharmacological duds that…"

"Wow," Jillian interrupted. "You said that word correctly!"

"Ha, ha. I am a writer, you know. As I was saying, they've created so many duds that I'm inclined to think they need to get out of the drug-making business altogether."

"I'm predicting they'll be filing for bankruptcy within the year," Vance said.

"You're probably right. I…" I trailed off again as I noticed my two dogs. "What are they looking at now?"

Sherlock and Watson had suddenly jumped to their feet and were staring at a hallway leading deeper into the Masters' home. Had they smelled something? Heard something? Well, as you'll see shortly, it turned out to be a little bit of both.

"What's with them?" Vance asked.

Just then, I saw Denise gently jab her elbow in Jason's stomach.

"It's your turn. I have a feeling she's awake. Sherlock and Watson must be able to hear her."

"I'll bet they can smell her," Randy added, with

a grin.

"They must be able to hear and smell who?" I wanted to know.

Jason silently rose to his feet, gave me a wink, and headed down the same hallway my dogs were focused on. After a few moments, he was back, only he was holding something. A furry, orange and white something. Jason placed the fuzzy form on the floor and took a few steps back. Intent on seeing what the object was, Sherlock and Watson crept forward.

"So, that day we met your two dogs," Denise began, as she rose to her feet and then knelt on the ground by the orange and white fluffball, "we just knew we had to have one. Therefore, Jason and I began calling around to see if there were any corgi breeders in the area. As it turns out, there were several, and one of them had puppies for sale. Only one was left, though, and that was because the breeder had classified her as a fluffy. Apparently, fluffy corgis aren't as desirable. I, for one, disagree. We both fell in love with her the moment we saw her. So, I'd like you all to meet our new puppy!"

The fuzzy puppy rose to her feet, shook herself a few times, and then noticed there were two adult versions of herself standing nearby, giving her curious looks. The puppy yipped once, bounded forward until she was sitting directly in front of Sherlock, and raised a paw, as if she expected to shake hands with the strangers. Sherlock cocked his head once, then twice, and then a third time. Then Sherlock yipped playfully and took off like a shot. The puppy barked excitedly and scrambled off in pursuit.

"Better get going, girl," I told Watson. "You're gonna be left behind."

Watson licked my hand once, as if thanking me for giving her permission to play, and ran off after the other two.

"She's adorable," Jillian gushed, as she turned to Denise. "And you're right. She's absolutely beautiful. I love how the markings on her face resemble that of a fox. Have you picked out a name for her yet?"

Denise smiled and nodded. "We have. We decided to name her Keeley. Keeley the corgi."

AUTHOR'S NOTE

Anyone familiar with what has been happening with me over the past few months will know why I threw in that last bit about the Masters' new puppy and why I chose that particular name. For those that don't, then I need to warn you that I'm about to impart some sad news.

My sweet little Keeley, my faithful companion for over 11 years, passed away several days after Thanksgiving, 2018. My wife and I were enmeshed in the packing/sorting of our Lake Havasu house and were spending one last week there to get everything out. Unfortunately, Keeley took a turn for the worse, and I had to make a decision that every pet owner dreads.

Okay, enough dreary news. Now, on to some good news. We have a new puppy, and her name is Kinsey. Wow. What a handful. I don't remember caring for a puppy being so difficult, only when I mentioned that to my wife, she not-so-kindly pointed out I was 11 years older. That shut me up.

What's next for me? Well, it's time to wrap up the Pirates of Perz trilogy. I left off with it being almost halfway done. I should be able to get that done fairly soon. Then it'll be another trip to Pomme Valley, and then? We're going to be heading to Cazel to see how Doiron is faring. Who's he, you ask? Well, if you haven't read Senthyd, a short story I wrote in 2016, then look me up on Facebook, or stop by my website, and ask me for a copy. I'll send one your way.

Senthyd was my first attempt ever at dipping my toe in the dark fantasy genre. Surprisingly (for me), it was received well and enough people asked about it, so it'll be developed into a full-length novel. So, I'm guessing that'll happen sometime later this year.

As for Lentari, I can tell you that no, the stories aren't done. I've got several other possible plotlines to explore, so it's just a matter of picking which one sounds the most interesting, and then it will be fleshed out into a story. I'm also working on a side project, based in Lentari, and will be ready to test it out soon. Yeah, I said 'test'. Think about that for a while!

That's about it for now. I'm off to start packing. Again. We're moving from our first apartment in Phoenix to a much nicer downtown location in just a few weeks. Yes, I can't wait, but egad, moving again???

J.
February, 2019.

THE CORGI CASE FILES SERIES

What's next for Zack and the corgis?

When Zack's girlfriend Jillian Cooper purchases one of Pomme Valley's historic properties, Highland House, little does she know a violent murder happened there over 70 years ago. Rumor has it that Dame Highland's ghost walks the halls, guarding her long-hidden treasure. Jillian wants to move forward with her plans to turn the historical house into a bed and breakfast. However, when an "accident" claims the life of a contractor, it becomes apparent that someone doesn't want people snooping around the house.

Can the canine crime fighters, along with their pack of humans, put a stop to the shenanigans before another tragedy happens? Don't miss the *Case of the Highland House Haunting*!

Sign up for Jeffrey's newsletter on his website to get the latest corgi news: www.AuthorJMPoole.com

<u>Available in e-book and paperback</u>
Case of the One-Eyed Tiger
Case of the Fleet-Footed Mummy
Case of the Holiday Hijinks
Case of the Pilfered Pooches
Case of the Muffin Murders
Case of the Chatty Roadrunner
Case of the Highland House Haunting
Case of the Ostentatious Otters
Case of the Dysfunctional Daredevils
Case of the Abandoned Bones
Case of the Great Cranberry Caper

Made in United States
Orlando, FL
07 January 2022

12973142R00168